WHEN SHADOWS FOLLOW

CALLIE RAE

For my Granny.   I hope you're proud.

CHAPTER ONE

The sound of an old bell echoes all around me as I stare at the school. It could have been built before my grandparents were ever even thought of. Two levels of solid weathered red brick with white columns around the arched main entrance are the only things standing between me and a fresh start—a fresh start that I want to run from.

"Honey, staring at it won't make it go away," my mother says through the passenger window, leaning from the driver's seat of her beat-up faded green minivan that's about one mile away from expiring. When we bought it, it was the only vehicle in our price range that was bigger than a skateboard.

I glance back at her as her eyebrows knit together. My mother has always been a pretty woman. Her shoulder-length blonde—now slightly grayer—hair frames a proportional face complete with steely blue eyes and a small, pointed nose. She has thin lips, with a few more wrinkles around her mouth and eyes than I care for, knowing I put them there.

"It will be okay, Fallon. We'll make this work. I promise," she says, trying to look reassuring. She sees the concern etched on my face.

I face the school, closing my eyes while I breathe in slowly. I hold it as I count to five before releasing it into the air along with the build-up of stress in my body.

"I have to go. I'll see you here at four?" I hitch my bag up my shoulder, checking back with my mom.

"I'll be waiting. Have a great first day. I love you," she smiles, then rolls up the window before driving away.

I stare at the school again. My view from the sidewalk has my stomach in knots.

"It has to work out," I say out loud to myself as I force my feet to move forward. "We're out of options."

The inside of the school is nothing like the outside. While the exterior is extremely outdated, the interior is entirely modern. The front lobby has marble floors and high ceilings. There is a statue of an old man off to the left, with a plaque inscribed with a name and the word "Founder" engraved underneath. To my right, there is a sign on a fancy stand that says "Main Office" in swirly letters with an arrow pointing towards a door not far from the entrance.

I step in front of the same door, staring at the words "Main Office" in frosted letters across the glass; it opens to a world I'm not sure about. It seems like I'm playing "What's Behind the Door" a lot lately. Let's hope I pick the right one this time.

Hoping it will calm my worried mind, I breathe in deeply. It doesn't help, but I take the step anyway and grasp the handle. Just as I push, the door is pulled away from me. I fall forward, bracing myself for impact with the floor, but it never comes. Large hands grip me by the arms. I glance up to see who's fortunate enough to catch me, but what I find are the most piercing dark eyes I have ever seen. They are almost black, but consumingly beautiful.

"Hey, you alright?" A deep, husky voice asks, jarring me from my swim in this stranger's eyes. I find my footing and straighten myself, taking a step back from his steady hands. I get a good look at my hero. He can't be much older than me. He has short, messy dark hair, a bar piercing through one of his bushy eyebrows, and a day's worth of stubble over his strong chin. Looking at his body, I'd guess he plays some kind of sport. He isn't too big, but his shoulders are broad, and his arms are defined. Black ink swirls over his knuckles, working its way up his forearm.

What else is hiding under his white shirt?

I bring my gaze back to his and swallow thickly, something in his swirling eyes pulls at me. Anger, or sadness? Maybe both?

I clear my throat, rasping out what I believe sounds like a yes.

"Ok, cool. So, can I . . .?" he says as he gestures towards the doorway I'm currently blocking, frozen in place.

"Oh! Yeah, sorry," I shuffle to the side with fidgety hands, allowing him to pass, but my eyes betray me as they follow him until he disappears down a hallway.

"Excuse me, can I help you?" A raspy voice speaks from behind me, but it takes me a long minute to register that the voice is speaking to me.

I reluctantly turn away from the direction the boy went to meet the stare of an older woman with smoky-gray hair standing behind a chest-high counter. The prominent lines are the first thing I notice about her face. They appear earned, like the wisdom in her bones is worn proudly through lines of honor. But her weathered skin is pulled tight, almost like leather, likely from years of smoking.

"Yes, I'm Fallon Blake. I'm looking for a . . . Mrs. Tate?" I say as I quickly pull a sheet of paper out of the side pocket of my bag. It has all of the instructions I wrote down for my first day.

"That would be me, Miss Blake. I have your schedule and locker combination ready for you." She grabs a folder with my name clearly labeled on the front.

"Your locker number is 159. Your combination is on the inside of the cover of your student handbook. I would advise reading the handbook entirely, as we have a full dress code and a strict plagiarism policy." She takes a small booklet from the folder opening the front cover to show me the combination, then places it back in the folder as it was. She pulls out a few sheets of paper from the front pocket, placing them in front of me.

"This is your schedule. Your homeroom class is Art History with Coach Henry. His classroom is room 205, on the second level. At the end of the hallway take the stairs to the second floor. It will be on the left. There is a map here to help you get around to each class.

We have an open lunch policy. You can leave the campus, but you are required to be back for the next class, or we will consider you skipping. Any questions?" she asks, as she neatly places all of the papers back into the folder with the student handbook. When I don't answer right away, she peers up at me through her eyelashes, raising her eyebrows expectantly.

"No, thanks. I think I can manage." I force out an answer, fighting through the flight response racing through my body.

"Well, good. Let me know if I can do anything for you. Your teacher is expecting you." I take the folder and turn to leave, but midway to the door, Mrs. Tate calls out for me, making me pause.

"I must advise you, because of your previous . . . situation, to choose your company wisely," she tells me nonchalantly—as if she isn't giving me a cryptic warning ten minutes into my first day of school.

I go in search of my first class, finding it right where she directed me. My heart starts pounding in my chest when I reach the classroom door. I watch a short, stubby man standing at the front of the classroom through the glass pane embedded in the door. He's pointing to something on the board. It's kind of ironic to me that a coach is on the heavier side.

I prepare myself to walk through the third life-changing door of the day. Again, I question if this is the right move for me.

With a sigh, I open the door and enter the class.

Like I have any other choice.

CHAPTER TWO

The morning passes slowly. The classes are ticking by, and I have a ton of homework to complete already. You'd think the teachers here would go easy on the new kid, but that's not the case. And I've spent more time today staring at the school map than actually learning something, which hasn't been the slightest bit helpful.

I'm wandering the halls looking for the cafeteria, which is what the map calls the commons area. It seems like it's at the back of the school and opens out towards the parking lot, but I'm not sure how I get there from wherever here is. I drop the map to my side, giving up on lunch—or even finding my way out of this building.

"Are you lost?" A soft voice has me quickly turning back. Standing in front of me is a dark-haired girl with long, braided pigtails and large gold hoop earrings. She's watching me curiously. So much for the dress code. The way her fitted shirt shows her midriff is definitely not in the handbook. She has make-up carefully placed around deep brown eyes. Eyes that I feel like I've seen before.

She looks at me impatiently, shuffling to her other foot. Right. She asked if I'm lost.

"Yeah, I'm looking for the cafeteria. I mean . . ." I look down at the stupid map again. "Commons area?"

"It's this way." She yanks the map out of my hand as she walks by. She goes to the nearest staircase, totally in the opposite direction I was heading. She doesn't check to see if I'm following as she tosses the map in a trash can conveniently located next to the stairwell opening.

She's pretty much my only hope at finding the cafeteria, so I rush to catch up with her. She glances at me several times as we walk, and I pretend I don't notice at first. But after the fifth or so time she has to know I can see her.

A sigh slips past my lips, "Go ahead and ask."

Her eyes widen, "What?"

"Whatever it is you want to know. Ask me."

She clears her throat.

Here we go.

"So, you're the new girl? Fallon, right?"

"Yep. It's my first day." *How does she know my name?*

"Jade." She points to her face.

"Don't worry, I'm not a stalker. Word gets around fast here. So, where'd you transfer from?" We turn a corner and enter an open area where several round tables with red stools attached are placed throughout.

"If word gets around fast, then shouldn't you know already?" I say, mocking her words from earlier and purposely deflecting her question. I'm not ready to freely give out my life story to anyone.

She chuckles, "Ha! Yeah, I guess so."

She leads me towards what I assume, based on the number of people lining up to a doorway, is the lunch line.

Jade smiles and waves at someone at the front of the line. She looks back at me to check that I'm okay. I nod, encouraging her to join her friend and leave me. I prefer to stay in the shadows anyway.

I wait in the back of the line. But when I make it to the counter, my stomach rolls with nerves at the sight of all the food. It's about as unsure of this new adventure as I am. I grab an apple to snack on and look for a place to sit in the crowded commons. Instead of fighting to find a seat, I go through the double doors that lead to the parking lot. There's a grassy area between the building and the parking lot where a few other students are sitting. I spot a corner where the building makes an L around the grass, and I sit down, propping my back up on the brick. I pop my headphones on, hoping the music will drown out my thoughts for a little while.

I people watch the different groups of my classmates as they carry on with their lunches, some leaving and some hanging around. I spot the black-eyed guy that caught me this morning, who I think is named Jesse. I overheard some girls gossiping about a guy in one of my classes, and their description matched him almost to a T. He is sitting on a bench attached to a picnic table with his arm draped across Jade's shoulders. It's a cozy little scene until she knocks his arm off of her.

Jesse suddenly becomes alert as he straightens, discarding his conversation with Jade. His smiling face and joking eyes from only a few moments before are now masked; his expression is void of any emotion. I push my headphones back and follow his line of sight to a guy walking up from the parking lot. This guy's brows are pulled down and he's glaring at Jesse. He doesn't look too friendly to me.

"Callaway! You have some nerve coming on my turf last night. You think you can just put your hands on my girl and walk away?" the guy shouts at Jesse. He's loud enough to be heard by anyone in the vicinity.

Jesse's visitor seems to be a few years older than us; he's probably two years out of high school. He's almost as tall as Jesse, but leaner with a shaved head. I can see a tattoo peeking out from under the collar of his shirt, rising up onto his neck. This guy looks like he could've come straight out of a rap music video.

Jesse crosses his arms over his chest. His head is lifted high, and he squares his shoulders as he lands Neck Tat with a hard stare. I think the corner of Jesse's lip twitches up slightly when Neck Tat plants himself right in his face, but it's gone before I can be sure. I wonder if he likes confrontation as much as I hate it?

"Last time I checked, your girl was on *my* jock—not the other way around," Jesse says, completely unperturbed. I look at Jade, but she seems unaffected by his admission. Their relationship confuses me.

"Yeah, we'll see about that. Come on my turf again, and you won't walk out. You feel me?" Neck Tat shuffles on his feet, shaking a bit of nervous energy out. He is obviously amped up.

Jesse stiffens at Neck Tat's threat and steps slowly, closing the little space left between them, bringing them nose to nose. His clenched fists drop to his sides as he leans forward, forcing Neck Tat to lean back enough to peer up at him. His manipulation of the situation is impressive, but I have a feeling that Jesse is itching for Neck Tat to hit him.

"Careful," Jesse growls through his teeth. "It would be a real shame if your pops found out what you've been moving on the weekends using his company trucks."

Shock flashes over Neck Tat's face. It is subtle, and he quickly recovers, schooling his features back into the "I'm a badass" attitude he brought with him. A smile tugs at Jesse's lips.

You caught that too, Chief?

"This isn't over Callaway. I'm coming for you. I'll get you where it hurts! Best believe that," Neck Tat sneers.

He spits at Jesse and starts to back away, but lifts both hands up as two other guys appear next to Jesse.

"I can't wait," Jesse says, low and steady. A frown appears on his face as he watches Neck Tat walk away, freely giving Jesse his back.

Jesse catches me watching him when he turns to face his friends again. He narrows his eyes and looks me over. I put my headphones back on as he watches. I lean my head back against the wall and close my eyes, hoping that will be the last exchange I have with him, or anyone else at this school for that matter. I don't need to be seen.

The rest of my week is seriously uneventful. Most of the student population has avoided the new girl, and I can't say that I mind. I sit in the same corner in the grass at lunch every day listening to my music. Today is no different. I find my way to my corner, put my headphones on, and soak in the sun.

Being left alone isn't in the cards today, though. A shadow falls over my face. I peek out of one eye to see what could be blocking the sun and find Jade awkwardly standing over me with a frown on her face. I haven't spoken to her since she showed me to the cafeteria. I sigh and push my headphones down around my neck.

"You need something?" I ask

She rolls her eyes, "There's a party tonight. It's at one of the players' houses. You should come."

I can't decide what her game is.

"Yeah, I'll get right on that." The sarcasm pours out as I go to put my headphones back on.

"Look—it's a prep party, but it has free beer and decent music. Just think about it, okay? Most of the school will be there." Jade pulls a piece of paper and a pen out from her bag, then writes something down. She holds it out to me when she's done. "This is the address and my number if you change your mind."

"Why are you here?" I look past her, not surprised to find Jesse watching our exchange.

She looks over her shoulder before shrugging. "People want to see what the new girl is all about. I'm the only one who has balls enough to come over here."

I grab onto the paper, but I stop before I pull it out of her hand. I have no intention of showing up at this party. "Tell these people don't bother. There isn't much to know."

She nods and releases the paper from her hold. I track her retreating figure as she walks back to her group of friends at the picnic table. She shakes her head at someone, but Jesse's glare at me over her shoulder interests me. I'm not sure what his problem is, and I can't allow myself to care. But I can't seem to pull my eyes away from him, either. I tilt my head and raise my eyebrows. I'm met with his smirk.

I see you, Chief.

The bell rings, and a blonde guy nudges Jesse's shoulder, but he doesn't move right away. Eventually, he breaks our stare and heads inside with his friend. I slowly put my headphones into my bag, trying to let the crowd thin out before heading through the double doors. Or maybe I'm just letting a particular crowd disappear first.

At final bell, I can't get to the front of the school fast enough. I'm hoping my mom is already here, waiting to pick me up. I find the ugly

13

green minivan right away—not that you could miss it in the middle of all the nice cars lined up. I avoided getting my license last year, leaving my mom as my only source of transportation. Unless I want to ride the bus.

And I so don't want to ride the bus.

As soon as I open the passenger door, my mom bombards me with questions about my day. She means well, but she can be a bit too much at times.

"So . . . any big plans this Friday night?"

I roll my eyes at her. "Mom, you know I don't have any, and even if there was something happening, I wouldn't go."

My mom regards me for a second, then she smiles from ear to ear. "There is something, isn't there? What is it?"

I groan. I should've known she would see right through me. "Yes, I was invited to a party. But it doesn't matter. I'm not going."

"Honey, you're seventeen. You still get to be a teenager. It's fine. You should go. At least try to make a friend here. I don't want you to be alone during your senior year. This is supposed to be the best year of high school."

"Mom I don't—"

"I don't want to hear it. You can, and you will. Now, where is this party?" She gives me her no-nonsense look, and I know she's made her mind up for me. She puts the van in drive as I pull out the piece of paper Jade gave me, handing it over. Most moms would be happy that their teenage daughter didn't want to go to a party, but not mine. She tries her hardest to give me that authentic teenage experience. It's out of guilt. But I don't get to be a typical teenager. Not now.

CHAPTER THREE

I brush my straight, light brown hair and watch in the mirror as it settles down to the middle of my back. I am as dull as it comes. I wish I looked more like my mom; my bust is fuller, my hips are broader, and my face is rounder. I'm oh-so graciously blessed with prominent features, just like my sperm donor; I refuse to call him my father. The only discernable feature on my face that I inherited from my mom are my high cheekbones.

I sit on my bed to pull on my Converse. I'm not dressing up for a house party. It's not like I usually dress up anyway. I'm wearing a simple outfit: my favorite pair of skinny jeans and a fitted white tee.

I sit back up and take a moment to just breathe. I look down at my forearm, focusing on the small tattoo of a moon near the bend in my elbow. I run my thumb across it, letting it calm me.

"Come on, Fallon. It's time to go." My mom's voice drifts in as she yells from across the house. I pull my jacket on and zip it up. I'm as ready as I'll ever be.

I hate parties. I always have. I had a boyfriend on the football team once that always wanted me to go to these things. I think he just needed to keep up appearances though; he would ignore me most nights to hang with his friends, only to come find me when he was ready to go.

I have my mom drop me off around the block to avoid any funny looks. I mean, who has their mom drop them off at a party? I'm greeted with a two-story house that looks like it should be in a magazine when I approach the address Jade gave me. The wrap-around porch and navy blue shutters give it a southern look. I'd stopped walking at some point. We're definitely not on my side of town anymore. Every house in this neighborhood is much nicer than our little two-bedroom home.

People have gathered onto the porch, and through the windows I can see groups scattered throughout the interior of the house. I hesitate, wanting to just turn around. *This is a bad idea.* I swear I can feel the air becoming thick around me, and my body's flight response kicks in.

"Shit. I can't do this," I say under my breath. I turn around to escape from my bad choices and begin to consider my options for getting home.

"Fallon? Is that you?" a familiar voice calls out, and I squeeze my eyes shut. *Crap.* I've missed my opportunity to run.

"Yep, here I am," I say as I spin back to the house. Jade is standing on the porch by the stairs. I'm surprised by her appearance: she's in a low-cut dress and heels that make her at least half a foot taller. It's a far cry from her boots and skinnies.

"You came."

"Yeah, I did." I nod my head up and down like an idiot.

"Come on, we have a keg in the back," she says over her shoulder as she starts walking towards the front door. I walk up the stairs and pass through the open doorway into a crowded living room. People let her slide through quickly. I stick close to her to avoid being swallowed by the sea of hormones.

I scan faces out of habit. I don't do well in crowded spaces. The music is so loud I can't think straight. *This is a horrible idea.*

She brings us to a kitchen that, despite being bigger than my entire house, feels homey. I watch as she grabs the top cup off a stack on the counter.

"So, what will it be? Beer or Vodka?" She says as she faces me, raising her voice a bit to be heard over the music.

"How about water?" I yell back.

"Uh, yeah. Sure. There's some in the fridge." She moves towards the fridge, and I turn to face the party. Leaning against the counter to hold me up, I see Jesse and his friend, who I think I have calculus with, walking through the crowded living room. Heading towards me. The crowd parts for them, much like they did for Jade. People are moving quickly to get out of their way. One girl rubs her hand down Jesse's chest as he passes. He doesn't even acknowledge her as he brushes past her. I'm not sure if it's the dominance he exudes, but it's clear as day who runs this show.

"It's a bit much, huh? The way they all worship those boys." Jade hands me a bottle of water and leans on the counter next to me.

"What's their deal?"

Jade takes a moment before answering me.

"Let's just say they inherited a lot of power." Her eyes tighten, and she almost appears sad as she takes a sip of her beer.

"Are y'all together?" The thought escapes my mouth before I can stop it. I turn to her just in time to watch her choke on her drink and dissolve into a coughing fit. Jesse just happens to reach us then and wraps her in a hug, making it worse.

"You alright, sis?" His face is full of concern as he lets go of Jade and pats her on the back. She coughs a few more times.

"I'm good," a slight hoarseness to her voice, "Jesse, this is Fallon. Fallon meet Jesse . . . my twin brother." My eyes widen almost instantly. My neck is suddenly very hot, and I can feel the heat rising to my cheeks.

"And this is our annoying cousin, Cason." Jade shoves the messy-blonde-haired, blue-eyed god in the shoulder. I watch as a muscular arm reaches back across and ruffles Jade's hair.

Is every guy at this school gorgeous and in shape?

"We've met," Jesse replies, seemingly indifferent, not mentioning my almost-fall. Jade's brows furrow, but she refrains from asking.

The dark tee and baggy jeans Jesse has on make his eyes appear a shade of black I've never seen before. His style screams "I don't care," but I think that's his appeal. He could make a brown paper bag look good.

He whispers in Jade's ear before grabbing two cups and walking off in the direction of the keg.

"You're the new girl, right? You're in my calculus class," Cason asks, and I glance up.

I gather my thoughts a bit before responding. He asked if I was the new girl, right?

"This is my first week at Cherry Creek," I say.

Jesse appears again, now with full cups, and hands one over to Cason. His natural frown is in place as he watches the party. He always looks so angry.

I'm not very inconspicuous as I watch him, and he catches me staring. I don't try to hide it. There is no point now that he knows I'm looking. The familiarity of the pain he hides under all of that control hits me in my gut.

What did he go through that could reflect my own pain right back at me?

My hand twitches as an itch to reach for him becomes nearly unbearable.

A guy pops his head through a side door in the kitchen that must lead to the backyard and I jump, breaking the moment. I shake my head to get rid of the thoughts I have floating around in there. That is the last thing I need.

He looks around, stopping when he sees Jesse and Cason. "You wanna play beer pong? They set up the table in the back."

Cason looks to Jesse with the biggest grin, and Jesse matches it with his own. He nods and they both run out the door like children.

I'm silent for a while until I can't hold in the awkwardness any longer. "So, your brother, huh?"

Jade chuckles. "Yep." She draws out the p with a *pop*.

But then she sighs. Giving me a little more insight, she says, "I look like our mom, and he looks like our dad. No one would know we were even related, let alone twins, if we hadn't lived here all our lives."

I nod as a bead of sweat forms on my temple. The party has grown so much that the crowd is now spilling over into the kitchen, leaving us surrounded by people.

Jade faces me, easily startling me. My anxiety really has me on edge.

"Jesse doesn't date." She tilts her head, studying my reaction. I don't give her one; it doesn't matter to me. I don't date either.

"Why are you telling me this?" I narrow my eyes as I wait for her to answer me.

"Because if that's why you came tonight, then forget it. It won't happen."

"Good thing it's not then, isn't it?" I lock eyes with her so she could see the seriousness behind my words. She nods before she breaks free from my gaze, turning back to the party as she takes a sip of her drink. And somehow, I think we might become friends.

CHAPTER FOUR

I push off the counter, reaching my limit when a girl in stilettos trips, sloshing her drink on my jeans. If I don't get out of here soon, I'll end up in full-panic mode. I can feel the anxiety bubbling up, and I start feeling woozy. It is trying to consume me.

"I think I need some air," I tell Jade, not bothering to wait for a response. I'm damn near running out of the same door the boys went through earlier in search of a bit of space. I step out onto the porch, which I would bet wraps around the entire house. I grab onto the railing with shaky hands and suck in a deep breath. My eyes close, and I count to five, then twenty. I need to relax. I look out onto the yard below me, hoping for a distraction. Off to the right a few guys stand at a table with cups lined up. This must be their beer pong table. I note that Jesse and Cason are missing. There's a few people sitting around a fire lit in the back corner of the yard. They're all laughing and having a good time; no one appears to have any cares at all. That used to be me, once upon a time. It feels like a lifetime ago.

Shouting jars me from my thoughts, and one of the guys at the beer pong table picks up a full cup. The other team must have made a ball. I laugh; the game you win by losing. I wish life could work that way.

I hear another shout. This time it sounds like it's coming from the side of the house. I look around to see if anyone else heard it, but everyone's going on about their business. Something has my feet carrying me towards the noise before my brain can talk my body out of it. I will probably regret this later, but I walk down the steps anyway. I'm watching my step when I hear a shuffling sound. I look up and stop short. Jesse and Cason are side by side, facing off with two guys. It doesn't appear to be a friendly meeting, either. I recognize one of the unwelcome visitors as Neck Tat, the same guy who confronted Jesse at school earlier this week. He has a friend with him this time. The guy looks like he came straight from prison, with crappy ink all down his arms and hands. His baggy jeans barely cover his boxers, and a plaid button-down is open over a tee shirt that must have been white at one time but now appears a sad shade of dishwater grey. Neck Tat and Prison Tat make quite the trashy-looking pair.

"Leave, Jax. Don't fuck with us here," Cason says. He sneers, showing his teeth in disgust.

"Now, boys. We're just here for a little fun, like everyone else," Jax says. He waves his hand towards the party.

"You heard him. Leave." Jesse says, stepping forward. Jesse's eyes never leave Neck Tat, but as soon as Cason steps in line Jesse shifts, all too aware of his surroundings.

Prison Tat's either brave or stupid, but he speaks anyway. "Jax, I don't think we're wanted here. Jesse, you would know all about being somewhere you aren't wanted, wouldn't you?"

"Why don't you stand there and shut up like a good little boy." Jesse's nostrils flare, his patience clearly thinning.

One side of Neck Tat's mouth perks up as he inches closer. "Tell me, Jesse. How is your sister?"

Jesse doesn't seem to react to Neck Tat's taunt, but his body tenses at the mention of his sister. I can see the vein protruding from his neck pulsing from here. These are his only tells; the mask he's using to maintain control of the situation is solidly in place.

Jesse slowly leans into Neck Tat's face, the move forcing him to take a step back. That one simple move changes the entire dynamic. Jesse's in control, not just of himself, but of Neck Tat and Prison Tat, too. They don't even realize it. With their backs so close to the porch, there isn't anywhere for them to go.

"I. Said. Leave." The threat is loud and clear. Even I cringe, his menacing voice sending chills down my arms.

Neck Tat swallows, and fear flashes in his eyes. He quickly hides it with a smile that anyone might believe if they didn't see the beads of sweat over his eyes or the way he repeatedly clenches his fist with a nervous twitch.

"I don't think I will. What you think, Ty? Are you ready to leave?" He glances at his boy.

Ty, which is apparently Prison Tat's real name, shakes his head. "Nah, man, I don't think I am."

Cason keeps his head forward, towards Ty, but he and Jesse together act like one machine. They are so in tune with each other that I almost miss it. The slight nod Jesse gives Cason is all the confirmation Cason needs for whatever he's going to do next. Once again, Jesse's controlling the game.

Cason holds his hands up and flashes a smile, his face lighting up like a damn Christmas tree.

"Fuck it, he warned you." He swings. His fist lands in Ty's face at the same moment Jesse leans in and lifts Neck Tat by the legs, effectively tackling him to the ground. They roll a few times until Jesse pops up, getting on top of Neck Tat and grabbing him by the throat.

The fight quickly turns as another guy appears out of nowhere and tackles Jesse off of Neck Tat. They both roll but pop up onto their feet. Neck Tat and the new guy now have Jesse cornered against the porch. New Guy reaches for Jesse, but he moves with ease as he blocks New Guy's advances. He wraps his arm around the back of the guy's neck and brings him down in a headlock. I swing my eyes to Cason and see he's still wrestling with Prison Tat on the ground. There is no way he's going to be able to help right now. I really want to walk away and let Jesse get pummeled. His issue with these guys isn't my problem to take care of. Everything in me is telling me to turn around and mind my business.

I curse under my breath. I should listen to the voice in my head and just walk away. But I'm a stupid, stupid girl. Instead, I look around for anything that could help. I spot a foot-long piece of pipe sticking out from under the porch and grab it. Inching forward, I stay close to the porch, using its shadows as cover. New Guy has Jesse around the waist, but Jesse's able to keep him in a neck hold. I hear a metallic clicking noise, and my head shoots up, making me pause. My heart drops a beat when I see what Neck Tat has pulled out of his pocket. He holds a switchblade out towards Jesse. Jesse's eyes are zeroed in on Neck Tat's hand and he's already yanking New Guy back to put distance between him and the knife.

My initial shock wears off and I slowly begin to move towards them again. Neck Tat's back is facing me; he's in the perfect position. When Jesse finally sees me, his eyes widen for a split second before he diverts them, so as not to bring attention to me. With a subtle shake of his head, he tells me in so many words to back off. I receive his message loud and clear. I should listen, but I won't. Especially when I see Neck Tat lunge towards Jesse with the knife. I'm a stupid girl, remember?

I take another step forward, erasing the last bit of distance between Neck Tat and me. I'm close enough that I could easily reach him. I send up a silent prayer before I take this last step. Jesse dodges the knife once more as I lift the pipe. His eyes nearly bug out of his head when he realizes what I'm doing. He pushes New Guy towards Neck Tat, causing him to jump back a few steps even closer to me. It was the perfect distraction to allow me to make my move.

I take a deep breath in an attempt to control my nerves and swing as hard as I can. Vibrations spread up through my arms when I make the connection with Neck Tats head. He drops in a slump at my feet. New Guy hits the ground shortly after with a grunt, barely conscious from the lack of oxygen. Jesse had managed to keep his arm wrapped around his neck this entire time. The guy's lips are blue.

I glance over at Cason. He's pushing Prison Tat's face down against the dirt, watching us. He gives me a curt nod, appreciation clearly written on his face. I look down at Neck Tat's body lying on the ground. I thought I would feel bad—or at least feel something, anything—after hitting this dude, but I don't. I'm numb.

A tug of my arm pulls my attention away. One of the hands that caught me earlier this week is gripping the metal pipe next to my side. Instinctively, I know I'll always know these hands. I bring my eyes to Jesse's. He's watching me, waiting for me to let go. There is no reaction to the fact that I just knocked a guy out with the same pipe he is trying to take from me. He brings his other hand up to my wrist and wraps his finger around it. His eyebrows lift, asking me to let go, and I slowly loosen my fingers.

As soon as the pipe is in his hand, he turns and pushes me behind him distorting my view of the trash on the ground.

"Find Jade and tell her to get the guys. She'll know what to do," Jesse says over his shoulder. He keeps his body turned towards the two guys on the ground in front of him. But I can't move.

He glances back at me realizing I haven't moved. "Go!"

This snaps me out of my frozen state, and I turn. At first, I walk, until walking turns into jogging, and pretty soon, I'm full-on running. I run straight into the house and push through all the bodies of people dancing until I find Jade right in the middle of the makeshift dance floor. I grab her arm, spinning her to face me and shout in her ear that Jesse needs help. Her eyes widen looking around the room. She moves quickly, grabbing several guys' attention. They all follow me through the back door, but once on the porch, they wait for me to direct them. I point to the side of the house, and they take off running.

Jade catches up to me, and we run. We find Jesse and Cason in the same position I left them in. When I get close enough, I hear Jesse's voice, "Grab your boy and leave before you find out what happens to druggies who don't listen."

I lift up on my toes to see through the group standing in front of me, looking for Jesse. I find him bent over the new guy holding his head up by the little hair he has on his head. He lets go, and New Guy's head bounces like a basketball on the hard ground, making me flinch. I look for the pipe, but Jesse no longer has it.

New Guy gets up and grabs Neck Tat by the arm, attempting to lift him. But he doesn't budge. Instead, he begins groaning as he rolls around on the ground. Cason slowly lets Ty up after mumbling in his ear. Ty helps New Guy lift Neck Tat off of the ground. Then they get into an old Chevy Impala that's still running. They knew they weren't staying, and I'd bet New Guy is their driver. They came here for one thing: to rile up Jesse. They get in the car and speed off, and relief floods me. It's over.

Jesse wastes no time barking orders. "Get everyone out."

Cason nods and heads inside. Just like that, he shuts down the party. It's not long before the music cuts off, and people start walking down the sidewalk. It doesn't get past me that when Jesse barks an order, everyone falls in line.

If he's kicking everyone out . . .

That means we aren't just at "one of the player's houses," as Jade put it earlier. This is *her* house, and if this is her house, then this is also *his* house.

With that, I start walking towards the road. I don't get too far before Jesse calls out to me, stopping me in my tracks.

"Not you, New Girl. You stay," he says. My shoulders tense almost immediately, and I grit my teeth as I turn around to face him.

Who is he, to talk to me like I'm one of his minions?

If he notices my glare, he doesn't let it be known. He just walks away. He leaves me standing there, watching his back recede toward the house.

"Just follow him, Fallon. Sometimes it's easier to just follow him," Jade says. Her eyes are drooping. She seems exhausted. She gives my arm a little tug as she passes me, and I reluctantly follow her.

I should've walked away when I had the chance.

CHAPTER FIVE

Jesse is standing at the door as we round the front of the house. He watches us come up the steps and holds the door open expectantly, like he knew I was going to follow. He impatiently bounces his leg as we file through the door. He's still amped up from the fight, but his jaw is ticking away in irritation.

And I'm not so sure it's not with me.

Those of us who are allowed to stay after Cason shut the party down gather in the kitchen. I find a spot against a wall at the back of the group. Out of sight of this cute little pow-wow.

"What the hell was that Jesse? I thought you were handling this?" Jade says to her brother as soon as he steps into the kitchen. I perk up. Things just got interesting; she is the last person I would expect to speak up.

"I'm. Handling. It. Jade. Stay out of it." Jesse's teeth stay clenched.

"Stay out of it? You just almost had your ass handed to you!" She's shouting now.

Jesse watches his sister lose her mind for a moment, and then his face visibly softens. "Jade, look at me . . . I'm okay."

Jade meets her brother's eyes, and their exchange draws me in even though it seems to be a private moment. But he's right. He has a small cut on his lip and a rip in his shirt, but other than that, he doesn't look too bad for someone who just fought off two guys.

Someone coughs, ending the moment carefully, and Jesse quickly looks up. Embarrassment flashes through his face when he realizes there's an audience. I decide this may be the best time to interject. I'm not standing here all night waiting for these people to figure it out.

"Not to ruin the moment, but can someone explain what just happened?" I'm hidden behind two very tall guys, but they move to the side to find the person behind the voice, giving everyone a clear view of me.

"It's none of your business, New Girl." Jesse says, his distaste for me apparent in the way he sneers when his eyes find me. There's no mistaking that it's just for me.

All right, Chief, I see you.

"It's Fallon. Or have you already forgotten? And the hell it isn't, I just saved your ass back there."

Jesse makes a very obvious pass over me with his eyes. The corner of his mouth lifts when he seems satisfied in what he sees.

Cocky bastard.

"That's cute, Fallon. So tell me, do you always do stupid things?" He tilts his head to the side, making me want to slap the smirk straight off his face.

"Stupid? You weren't getting out of that. They had you cornered," I say, now more irritated at myself for helping him.

I push off of the wall with my foot, stepping into his space. He reacts instantly, meeting me halfway. We're so close I can feel his warm breath sail across my face. He looks down his face at me and rolls his top lip, barring his teeth. "I had it under control."

I stand tall, lifting my chin while meeting his gaze. I refuse to let him throw his alpha male bullshit on me. "You were about to be put on your ass, and you know it. Next time I might just let you fall."

"Who says there will be a next time?"

It's my turn to look him over. I cross my arms and run my eyes down the length of his body, the same way he did mine. I let my disapproval be shown. "Oh, there will be."

"Jesse used to be friends with Jax, the one with the tattoo on his neck." Jade's voice cuts in, bringing us out of whatever dance we're doing. Everyone's eyes are darting between us. They look just as confused as I am about this exchange.

Jesse spins to his sister.

"Jade," he barks, "stop talking."

"This is your fault, brother. You brought her here!" She snaps.

What the hell does that mean?

With the way she's glaring at him, there is no way Jesse will get away with attempting to shut her down in front of all of these people. I'm beginning to think this girl just might have claws hiding in there.

Ignoring her brother's warning, she continues. "Jax got caught up with the wrong crowd. At first, it was just pot, but he got deeper and deeper until . . ."

Jesse releases a frustrated growl. "The one you hit is Jax. He has the hook-up for any of your drug preferences."

He drops his head forward, his hand rubbing the lines on his forehead. He's no longer fidgety, and I assume any adrenaline rush from the fight is long gone by now. He growls for the third time tonight as he swipes his hands down his face.

"And because you involved yourself tonight, it makes you a problem. He'll be looking for the person who hit him. He'll know it wasn't me, and we don't know what Ty saw. You should've minded your own business."

His words stir a storm inside of me, causing my pulse to jump, "I'm no one's problem. I don't want any part of this. I didn't even want to come tonight. Why am I even here? What kind of game are you and your friends playing here? You invite me to a party, but forget to mention it's at your house, that it's your party?"

I make sure to look directly at Jade on that last part.

"Well, it's a little too late for that now. You think he won't come back for revenge, New Girl? We aren't talking about rainbows and butterflies here. These guys would love to get their hands on a pretty little princess like you. Your best hope is that they didn't see your face."

I'm really getting tired of him growling at me, and he didn't answer any of my questions. Judging by the way his jaw is flexing and neck is pulsing, he isn't as in control as he would like everyone to think. I lifted the corner of my mouth in a smirk. He sees it, and his eye twitches slightly.

That's right, Chief, you don't fool me.

29

"But you gotta admit that swing was impressive man. Them little arms did some damage tonight. You can back me up anytime, Ruth." Cason smiles at me and reaches for my biceps, pretending to size them up. I let out a weak laugh at his antics.

"Wait, *she* put Jax on the ground? Damn New Girl, you got a helluva swing." A guy standing next to Cason offers his hand to me. I stare at it, not moving to take it, looking him up and down. He isn't a bad looking dude, but most of the guys at this school look like they walked off a photo shoot anyway.

"Keep your nose out my business, New Girl, and don't make any more stupid moves." Jesse interrupts the praise I'm receiving as he steps between me and this guy with a scowl on his face. He reaches into his pocket and pulls out a set of keys, tossing them to his sister. "Take her home."

He doesn't look to her. Instead, he keeps his eyes on me like I might run away—not that I haven't considered it.

"And don't talk about tonight with anyone."

I'm done with this entire situation. I roll my eyes as I walk out, saluting Jesse with my non-manicured middle finger before Jade can even acknowledge her ass of a brother's request. The cap on my anxiety is about to blow, and I have to ball my trembling hands into a fist to hide the effects from the panic attack I'm just barely keeping at bay. I catch the slightest echo of a chuckle before I cross the threshold of the front door.

I make it to the front porch without erupting like a volcano in front of everyone. I'm all too aware of how bad this situation can be. I didn't need to be caught up in their crazy drama. I have my own to deal with.

Jade chooses that moment to walk out onto the porch, but she averts her eyes, refusing to look at me. She doesn't speak either as she heads down the steps toward a black charger that I assume is Jesse's. I fall in step behind her, never more thankful to be going home than I am right now.

CHAPTER SIX

I'm not prepared to face the world when Monday morning arrives. Especially not after the weekend I had. I don't foresee any more parties for me in the future.

I walk through the halls of Cherry Creek High, and people are mumbling all around me. I feel the stares on me like ants crawling over my body as the whispers flutter over to me. The sea of people part as I continue to walk. But even when they move out of the way, I'm still the center of their focus, and I have no idea why.

The eerie silence that I face when I cross the threshold to my homeroom class has me faltering. I try to ignore it, hoping it will go away. I sit at my usual desk, but today I keep my head down to make myself as small as possible.

So much for being invisible.

"Psst. Psst!" A guy sitting in the row next to me is staring at me. I cut my eyes to him as I wait for his next words.

"I heard you and Callaway were getting along real well Friday night," he wiggles his eyebrows suggestively. I curl my fist as he high fives the guy sitting across from him.

I watch him. The dumb look I have on my face seems appropriate now.

Nope, nuh-uh, no.

I sigh. Please let this day pass quickly.

"Is that all you got? It's lame. Leave the sexual innuendos to the people who know how to spell the word sex," I say, and his laugh quickly turns into a frown. A slightly confused look crosses over his face. I widen my eyes, trying not to let the laughter bubble out.

Well, shit, he really can't spell sex.

"Half the school body wants to be you. The other half wants to screw you. There is a small percentage that may want to run you over," the girl sitting to my right whispers.

"What do you mean? Why?"

"You got everyone's attention. Just be careful of some of the girls here. They can be ruthless when they feel threatened. And they definitely feel threatened."

"I don't understand. I didn't do anything." I don't think I really want to understand the ways of the high school girls here. Something tells me they are savage.

"Rumor is there was a situation at Friday's party, and one new girl got to stay while everyone else was thrown out. No one from the outside is included when Callaway calls his crew together, and you just came out of nowhere. And now you're one of them. Jesse put his mark on you by letting you stay, whether you like it or not." She smirks at me as she looks me over.

"Oh, please. King Jesse didn't let me in on anything that matters, I promise."

"That's not what it looks like from their point of view," she tells me, pointing to two girls who are glaring from across the classroom.

"Which category do you fall into?"

She chuckles, "I certainly don't want to be you. I definitely don't want to screw you. And I want to run over everyone in this place."

Ok. She's a little demented.

"Thanks . . ." I don't know her name.

"Mira. Whatever. Just thought you needed to know what you got yourself into." She waves her hand but never looks back up from her textbook.

The stares and whispers don't stop. By lunch, I'm ready for this day to be over. I grab my food and head towards the double doors, itching to get away from everyone. Unfortunately for me, a few overly-jealous girls stop me from being able to disappear to my corner.

"What do you think you're doing?" A blonde chick with perfect curls and nails that would put a cat's claws to shame stands in front of me in her tiny cheerleading uniform. I count to ten in my head, trying to prepare myself for this. Nothing good ever comes from cheer bitches.

"I'm trying to enjoy my lunch. You couldn't tell?" I smirk, letting my annoyance show on my face.

"With Jesse, dumbass. You've been here for a week, and you just think you can do whatever you want?" This girl has mastered the evil glint in her eye. She probably scares most of the school population with it. I let out a sigh. My corner, where everyone leaves me alone, is literally ten feet from me. I will my body to appear there. I even close my eyes, hoping that when I reopen them . . . Nope, she's still in front of me, with no corner in sight.

Damn.

"Does this usually work for you? The whole bitchy queen attitude you have going on? I mean, you even brought your squad to confront me. That's cute. I'm going to let you in on a little secret—I don't give a fuck about your precious Jesse." I step into her personal space, making sure she understands how serious I am. "Now, go back to your little hero worship and move the hell out of my way." I walk through her little squad, making sure to shoulder check her.

"This is my school." I stop walking when her annoying voice finds me again. "I can make your life miserable. Stay away from him."

I glance over my shoulder at her tiny, peppy form. Her threat is empty to me. "My life's already miserable."

I don't know what the hell I did to deserve this kind of karma, but this day is getting worse by the second.

"What did she want?" I glance up to see Mira, following me.

"To warn me that Jesse is off-limits." I reach my corner and sit down, opening the bag of chips that came with my lunch.

She rolls her eyes and sits across from me. I look at her. *What the hell does she think she's doing?*

"She is such a bitch. Callaway messed around with her last year, and she thinks that she's the queen of Cherry Creek now." Mira pulls out a box of candy from her bag. "Let me guess—she told you she would make your life miserable if you didn't leave him alone?" she asks, popping a SweeTart in her mouth. "That's her M.O. She really needs to update her material."

"Something like that." I watch warily.

"A girl hooked up with Jesse at a party once, and Elizabeth stuffed her in her gym locker in nothing but her underwear. The janitor had to cut the lock off to get her out."

"Mira, what are you doing? Why are you warning me about those girls, and why are you sitting here?" I'm still staring at her.

"She was my friend. My only friend at this school, and they drove her to transfer schools. They're mean, and you seem like the kind of girl that will fight back. I just want to be around when it happens." I can respect her answer, but I don't like it. The rage is right there in her eyes; she means every single word.

I pull out my iPod, popping my headphones on.

Mira settles in on the opposite wall and I let the music block her and the rest of the world out.

I hope she can do silence, because that is all she'll get.

By Friday, the stares and whispers have died down. Apparently, some chick hooked up with one of the guys on the basketball team in the bathroom. They got caught when a teacher was passing by the bathroom door and heard her moan. She thought someone was hurt. I bet that was a surprise of a lifetime.

Although, the rumors have been impressive. At one point, I think I heard a girl telling her friends that I'm the Callaway twin's long-lost sister. That one made me laugh.

Mira has hung around all week. We don't talk much. I try to ignore her and she accepts my silence, for the most part.

"Hey, a bunch of us are going to the Depot this weekend. You wanna go?" Mira asks as she plops down next to me on the quad.

"Why would I want to do that?" I raise my eyebrow at her.

She shrugs, "It's pretty chill. Free booze. Besides, there's not much to do in this shit town."

"So, stay home," I tell her, pulling my headphones out of my bag.

34

Just like every day this week, she has a box of candy in her bag. She pulls it out and offers me some.

"You're going to have to face the world eventually. Might as well do it while having a little fun."

She would make a pretty damn good point—if I were a normal girl.

"No. Did you not hear the rumors about what happened at the last party I went to?" I shake the memories from my mind.

"Do you make a habit of hitting guys with poles?" She asks, sarcasm dripping from her voice. She cocks her eyebrow questioningly.

"No, but I don't make a habit of repeating the same mistakes either," I say.

"Whatever. I'm going to leave at about ten. If you change your mind, text me." She leans back when I put my headphones on. I'm ready to be enveloped in my music, to block out the thoughts, but her words repeating in my head keep me from getting lost like I wanted too.

You're going to have to face the world eventually.

I just don't want it to be any time soon.

I arrive home to a note from mom. She's working later than I expected. I knew she was working late when she texted me to take the cringe-worthy bus home, but I didn't think it would be this late.

Great.

I stand in the kitchen with old wood cabinets and just listen. It's so quiet. It shouldn't be this quiet; it was never supposed to be this quiet.

I bring my bags into my room and drop onto my back in my bed, looking at the discolored ceiling. I can tell there was a water leak at some point in here, because the roof is slightly browned in the corner with water stains.

I'm not prepared to be home alone tonight. I didn't plan anything for supper, so a sandwich it is. I have zero homework to do to keep me preoccupied. I grab my headphones and turn the music as high as possible. The silence is creeping in though, making me antsy. I finally give up, yank my headphones off, and pick up my phone.

Me: Fine. I'll go. Pick me up?
Mira: I knew you would.

35

Me: Yeah. Whatever. Are you coming or what?
Mira: You know it. Address?

I text her my address and go to my closet. My friends from before would say choosing an outfit is difficult, but it's not for me. I'm going with my go-to band shirt and jeans. I pull on my lace-up boots and grab my black leather jacket, just in case it gets chilly. Because I have no idea where we're going.

Mira pulls up in a silver SUV with two boys that look a few years younger already in the backseat. I climb into the passenger seat, trying to ignore the boys' eyes on me. I'd forgotten how the early teen years made boys little perverts.

"Sorry. This is Cory and Ryker. Just ignore them. They're my brothers. My mom made me bring them with me." She points to the back and rolls her eyes.

"Whatever, Mom wanted us to babysit you and make sure you don't do anything dumb." Cory huffs. "At least it's the Depot. We'll be able to have fun there."

I chuckle at their dynamic. I don't have siblings, but I think it would have been nice if I did.

"So. What exactly is the Depot?" I ask. Everyone stops talking, real fast.

"You haven't heard of the Depot yet? Jesus Fallon, you really do live under a rock." Mira's eyes widen. "The Depot is owned by your favorite person ever. Jesse Callaway."

I smirk at her. She thinks she's funny, but I'm not amused.

"Well, technically it's his father's, but they basically started it for Jesse. It's car races. It's legal for the most part. The only thing not legal about it is underage drinking. But if nothing gets out of hand, then the cops tend to leave it alone. I guess it's better than us running the roads."

"Great, so it's a big party with cars involved. Seems safe."

She laughs. "You have no idea."

Turns out, she was right. I wasn't prepared for the Depot. Not one bit. When we pull up, there are rows and rows of cars parked in a field. We find a spot in the last row in the very back, leaving us to make a small hike to get to the track.

There are groups of people everywhere. The crowd is wild. As soon as we walk up, they explode in cheers all around me.

Mira tells her brothers to get lost, and I follow her to a smaller group sitting around an older muscle car. We get about six feet from them when the catcalls start.

"Dang Mira, where did you find her?" a guy in her group of friends yells out. Mira walks straight up to the only other girl with them, ignoring the questions. She gives her a hug before punching the guy whistling at me playfully on the shoulder.

"I don't know if you want to mess with her. She's already on Callaway's radar," another guy snorts. I recognize him from the party the other night.

"Aw damn, that's her," the girl says, bringing my attention back to her. She has red low-lights striped through her black hair. She's wearing a tight top that covers so little it almost isn't necessary. She's naturally tan in a way most girls would be jealous of, and gives off a rough, no-nonsense vibe with her appearance. But something tells me it's just a cover.

"May I introduce you all to Fallon. Yes, she *is* the one who nailed Jax in the head with a pipe."

I roll my eyes at Mira. Her dramatics do nothing for me.

"Fallon, this is Jordan, Crank, Goose, and Narni," Mira says, pointing to each of them as she says their names.

Jordan reaches behind him into a chest on the ground once Mira's done with introductions. He hands over two beers, one each to me and Mira. I take the cheap can of cold piss that is likely to be the only thing I enjoy about this night and pop the top.

Here's to being seventeen.

A few deep sips of brew and I glance over Mira's friends. I have to admit they are pretty easy on the eyes if you like the rough-around-the-edges look. Piercings in their ears, tattoos all over. Goose even has them on his knuckles.

I take another sip of my beer. It still tastes like shit. But it'll do.

"Crank and Goose, huh? Do I want to know?" I ask.

Jordan laughs.

"Yeah, Crank here," he nods towards his buddy, "can fix anything that drives and Goose because he usually gets lost in some goose by the end of the night. If you get what I'm saying." He sends an exaggerated wink my way.

I almost spit my beer out. Somehow, I'm able to keep it all in my mouth without spraying someone with cheap beer.

"They nicknamed you after a vag?" I say. "That shit's hilarious."

Jordan smiles while I laugh. Everyone seems amused except Goose, who is cutting eyes at Jordan.

Mira cozies up to Jordan. His arm instinctively wraps around her, but his eyes roam over a girl's ass nearby. I decide I'm staying away from that mess, and I turn my back, facing the track to watch what all the hype is about.

Two cars are lining up at the starting line. They are so modified I can't even tell what make of vehicles they are.

"Hellman is not going to win this one. No way. Dude just doesn't have the horsepower," I hear Crank saying behind me.

It's all lost on me. I have no clue about anything car-related. I watch race after race. The next racers line up quickly after each race is over. Two of the most expensive cars of the night line up. I would be afraid to get a scratch on either of them.

A prickle on the back of my neck gains my attention. I look up into familiar black eyes—ones that I would know anywhere.

Jesse.

He's across the track, leaning on the front of his car, and his eyes are on me. The racers start revving their engines, but his gaze stays locked on me. His cousin Cason—at least, I think is his name—walks up next to him, slapping a hand on Jesse's chest. Jesse smirks, but still holds my gaze. Cason whispers something in his ear and a blur of white and red flash across my line of vision as the race begins. As soon as the cars pass, I look back for Jesse, but the spot on his hood is empty.

"Damn, girl. That look he just gave you is enough to make any girl drop their panties," Narni chuckles. She's observant, I see.

"Whatever. He's a rich prick that thinks he can control everyone," I say. I wrinkle my nose as I face Narni.

"That's because he does control everyone," Jordan interjects. "His dad controls this town, and young Jesse is following in his daddy's footsteps. He rules Cherry Creek High, and out here, he's in charge."

38

He cuts all playfulness from his tone. My spine tingles; he has a warning hidden in there, but for what I don't know.

"He doesn't control me." My teeth clench.

"Not yet, he doesn't." Jordan's hard stare meets mine. "Won't take long for him to control you too, guessing by the way he was staring at you just now."

He brings his beer to his mouth, still watching me over the metal, testing me.

"The look of disgust? Yeah, that'll get him far."

Jordan laughs. "You don't get it, do you? That look just now? He's accepting the challenge."

"What challenge? I don't play games like a toddler. How would you know anyway? I don't see you over there in his group?" My irritation is growing. Jordan narrows his eyes.

"Chill Fallon he's—" Mira starts, but Narni steps forward, getting real close to me.

"What Jordan is trying to say is *you* are the challenge. You're defiant and don't play by his rules. He's coming for you, and there's nothing you can do to stop it." Narni's voice is low and harsh. It's enough to make my insides vibrate.

I look past her, considering my next words. Thankfully Crank starts laughing, effectively breaking the tension.

I watch Narni closely, waiting to see what she's going to do. She begins to laugh too, and I relax. "It's all cool. We'll be nice while you're still around. Jordan get her another beer." She pats me on the shoulder before walking off behind me.

"Well, there she goes. Poor guy," Goose chuckles. We all look in her direction

"You think she'll ever settle?" Mira asks as Narni walks up to a random guy, flirting heavily.

"Nah, she's too fucked in the head. That would be way too normal for her," Jordan says, with no hesitation. There's something about him that doesn't sit right with me.

CHAPTER SEVEN

The races are decent entertainment. I learn that they're called drag races. The cars race on a straight track for a short distance, and whichever car can accelerate fast enough to get to the finish line first wins. According to Crank, most of the cars out here are pieced together and modified to go faster. Apparently, he's the local mechanic for many of the guys out here.

The stakes can be pink slips or cash. Most go for money, but every now and then, someone gets cocky enough to race for slips.

I'm told that Jesse's dad hired a woman, maybe in her early twenties, as the track manager since Jesse is underage and can't always be out here. They all advise me to steer clear of her because she isn't afraid to kick some ass. I think I would probably like her.

I saddle up next to Mira on the hood of the car. Jordan left with Goose to go fill up the ice chest at Goose's truck.

"Does Jesse race?" I ask.

She's quiet at first. I figure she's just contemplating how to answer.

"No, not anymore. Ever since . . ." She hesitates like she is debating how best to continue. "Some shit in his family went down, and he hasn't gotten back on the track since then."

Of course, my curiosity spikes at this, but I don't push for more. If Mira is protecting the truth, then it's not something that's talked about.

My phone starts ringing, and I dig it out of my back pocket to see my mom calling. I curse when I realize I didn't let her know I was leaving tonight. She's probably freaking out. I let Mira know and walk off towards the parking lot to get away from all of the noise.

"Hey, Mom, what's up?" I say into the phone.

"You weren't here when I got home, and I wanted to check on you. Is everything ok?" She sounds worried, and I hiss. I hate making her worry.

"Yeah, I'm really sorry. Mira, this girl from school, picked me up to bring me to some car races. I forgot to leave a note."

"Oh. You're out with a friend? I just wanted to make sure everything was ok. I'm so happy you decided to go out with friends."

"'Sup girl. Whatchu doin' out here all by yourself?" A guy's voice has my head snapping up.

"Hey mom, the races are about to start up again. I have to go. I shouldn't be out too much longer." I hang up before she can reply, knowing I might catch hell for it later.

"I'm good, just taking a phone call," I say into the dark. The person speaking steps into the light with two others behind him. Ice douses my head when I recognize him. It's Jax, the guy from the party.

I stand taller, straightening my spine, and I'm on alert. This isn't good. I don't know if this dude recognizes me, but thankfully his buddy Ty isn't with him tonight.

"Say, do I know you? You look real familiar." He tilts his head.

"Nah, I don't think so. I'm gonna head back to the races now." I point over my shoulder and start backing away. I fight the urge to turn and run.

He doesn't let me get far before his hand encloses around my upper arm. I close my eyes and curse myself for coming out here alone.

"Where you goin' so fast?" he spins me back to him and pulls on a strand of my hair that fell in my face. "What's your name?"

"Look, dude, I'm just here hanging with some friends. I don't know what you all are up to, but they're waiting on me, alright?" I try to sound more confident than I feel.

He drops his hand and makes a motion of holding them up like he's innocent. Of course, I know better. "Alright, alright. I ain't here to start no trouble. But before you go, can I get your name?"

"How about you get lost instead?" Jesse's steady voice comes from behind me, and for the first time, I'm happy he's here.

"Chill, Callaway. We're just talking," Jax says, acting dismissive towards Jesse. Even I know that was the wrong move.

"I said get lost, Jax." Jesse steps forward and reaches across my stomach, firmly gripping my hip and moving me behind him. He doesn't release me from his hold, even once I'm safely tucked away. My skin tingles where his hand lingers. I want to scream at my body for reacting to his touch. I want to hate it, just like my mind wants to hate him.

"Ah, I get it now. She's yours. Well, damn. Now I really wish I'd gotten her name." Jax laughs with a snap of his fingers. Jesse tenses up in front of me as his grip tightens on my hip.

"What's that phrase, an eye for an eye? You better watch it. Your girl, too," Jax sneers. People are starting to gather around us. Some have their phones out. Cason and Jade appear, flanking Jesse. Jordan and Goose stood behind us. Jordan is still holding his ice chest in one hand, but his grip is hard, and his knuckles white.

They're going to back Jesse up without question. Does he really have that much control over these people? Jax looks around, contemplating his next move. He has no ground out here. I think he knew that before he came. He was just looking for trouble, and he's gotten exactly what he was looking for.

Jax lifts up his hands and begins to back away, nudging his friends in the shoulder to follow him. He turns around when he's far enough away, walking off into the parking lot, as the darkness swallows him again.

Jesse doesn't waste any time rounding on me. "You're a fucking hazard. Why can't you stay out of trouble?"

"Me? You're the one with obvious beef with the guy. I didn't start this mess," I say. He's lost his mind if he thinks he's going to check me out here in front of this crowd.

"I didn't ask you to involve yourself. Do you not use your head? Do you think it's safe for a little girl like you to be walking out here in the dark by yourself?"

"I can take care of myself," I snarl.

"Obviously." He puts his face two centimeters from mine. I stop breathing when his cologne wafts up to my nose. It gives him a manly, musky scent that I can't deny does something for me.

"Stick close for the rest of the night. And do me a favor? Stop being stupid. I don't want to have to worry about saving your ass—again." He flexes his jaw.

Oh hell no.

"Not to interrupt this pissing match, but did you hear what he said? An eye for an eye. He thinks she's your girl now. I think y'all probably would have great hate sex . . . but yeah, he's going to come after her," Cason points out.

"I heard," Jesse snaps.

"So, what are you gonna do?" Cason asks.

"I don't know. Just keep an eye on her for now. I'll figure something out." Jesse rubs his hands through his hair.

"Uh, yeah, hello? I'm right here. Why don't you go back to ignoring me, and we'll call this a day? I don't need you to babysit me." My agitation with this dude is growing ten-fold.

Jesse snorts. "I didn't ask you. But if you want us to throw you to the wolves, I'll be more than happy too. Just don't come running back when they bite."

"I think I can deal. But thanks for the heads up." I walk off, not listening to any more of his crap.

I find Mira and tell her I'm ready to go, but she's more concerned with Jordan's tongue than taking me home. She sways a bit on her feet when she looks up. She's drunk, and there is no way she's driving me home. Jordan tells me he'll get her and her brothers back, no big deal. There's no concern about how I'll get home. *Great.* I refuse to call my mom; she worries about me enough.

I growl in frustration. This is why I keep to myself.

"You ok?" I glance up. Cason is standing nearby, watching me warily. I snarl, and he sticks his hands up in surrender. "Chill. If the bossman wants an eye on you, then I'm going to keep an eye on you. Might as well make it civil, right?"

He points to Mira. "You rode here with her?"

I glance over my shoulder to Mira stumbling a bit. Jordan's hands are the only thing keeping her from tumbling over.

"Yeah. But she isn't in any shape to take me home. Or herself, for that matter."

Cason nods. "Come on, I'll give you a ride."

I go to object, but he cuts me off before I can say anything. "It's just a ride. Don't overthink it. Besides, do you have a better option?"

He smirks, making me roll my eyes heavily. I look back to Mira again, who's back to sucking face with Jordan. Cason is my best option. I face him.

"Fine. Thanks," I grumble. He turns and begins walking to the parking area, and I follow.

Cason drives a Jeep. The kind that has four removable doors and looks similar to a tank, but tonight the doors are still in place. It's not a smooth ride, but it's still a nice one. As he pulls out onto the road, I rub my hand down the side of the black cloth seat. I smile to myself; the tan cloth in our ugly green van isn't nearly as kept up. I'm not really sure the interior was even tan when it first started out. It's probably faded from years of children and messes. I like to think that the previous owners were a happy, full family.

We stop at a traffic light, and Cason turns towards me. "Look, I don't know you. But I'm gonna go out on a limb here and say your tough exterior is just an act." He drums his fingers on the steering wheel. "I say that because Jesse is the same way. Don't get me wrong—he's tough, but he's not a bad guy." The light turns green, and we begin to move again.

I turn my head to look out the window. I will listen, but I don't have much I want to say about Jesse.

"What I'm trying to say is that I don't think you're a bad person either. I just think you're a little unlucky. I know Jesse sees that too, but he doesn't trust people easily."

My head whips to Cason, my eyes wide, and I raise my eyebrows at him. "Are you talking about the same dude that barks in your face like he's the king?"

Cason laughs. It's full-on, genuine hysterical laughter. And oh my, it's a pretty thing to witness. Judging by the worry lines on his face, I'm guessing he doesn't laugh freely like this very often.

"Yeah, I guess he doesn't really have great social skills, huh?" He laughs again as he throws his jeep into park in my driveway. Just as fast as his bright laughter came, his face goes solemn. "I know it's not much, but don't throw away the key yet. He's a good guy. He's also good to have on your side in Cherry Creek."

On that note, I jump out of the Jeep and turn back to face him, meeting his steady gaze with mine. "That's great and all, but I didn't ask him for any of this. I just want to be left unseen."

"If that were true, you would have never picked up that pipe. You want to be seen, but something has you keeping your guard up." Cason levels me with his glare, searching my eyes. His words hit me hard in my gut, and I'm unable to keep the truth off my face. He's right—if I'd really wanted to stay in the dark, I wouldn't have helped them. I swallow hard before I shut the passenger door and watch him back out of my driveway. It dawns on me then that I never told him where I live.

CHAPTER EIGHT

My phone buzzes from my bedside table, stirring me from a deep sleep. I check the time and rub my eyes a bit to clear my vision. It's a text from a number I don't recognize.

Who could be texting me so early?

Unknown Number: Get ready, picking you up in 10. Jade

How does she have my number?

Me: How did you get my number? And I have a ride, thanks.

Jade: Come on, Fallon. It's just a ride. My grumpy other half said to tell you that you have 7 minutes, or he WILL carry you out of the house in whatever it is you are wearing. 😊

I roll my eyes. I really believe he would, too. My mom would freak. Imagining that makes me chuckle. My phone beeps again.

Jade: Cason said he would get you coffee—the good stuff—if you play nice.

Me: Fine.

Jade: Great, see you in 5.

I drop my phone on the bed and rush to our bathroom to brush my teeth and hair. I throw on a pair of jeans and a t-shirt and grab my jacket. I get it halfway zipped up just as a loud rumble comes from outside my house, followed by a horn honking. I roll my eyes. Someone needs to check these people before I lose my mind on them.

"Fallon? There is a black car in our driveway honking. Some guy is hanging out the window yelling at the house. Do you know who they are?" My mom comes in my room wide-eyed.

"It's Jade, with her brother and cousin. They want to give me a ride today," I grimace.

"Oh. Well, what's wrong with that?" My mom has a little glint in her eyes. I can tell it's making her happy to see me with friends.

"Mom, you know why. I'm supposed to be keeping my head low and staying to myself. They are the exact opposite of that."

"Fallon, honey, you are allowed to be a teenager. We moved here to give you a fresh start. Not to hide you away from the world. Give this a chance—it may be good for you." The concern she's showing makes me want to throw all my worries out the window just to try to make her happy, but I don't know if I could handle putting her through anything else.

We both glance up when the horn honks two more times. I pick my bag up from off the floor where it landed after I finished my homework last night. I turn back to my mom and sigh. She watches as I resign myself to the fact that no one is giving me a choice in the matter. I find no point in arguing about it.

"I've got to go." I kiss her on the cheek and leave her sitting on the edge of my bed.

"Let me know if I need to come and pick you up this afternoon," she calls out to me.

Don't worry, Mom. I'm pretty sure he already has that planned out for me too.

The sun blinds me the moment I step outside. It takes my eyes a minute to adjust. But when they do, I'm not surprised to find Cason's head hanging out of the passenger window like a dog with his tongue out. I shake my head at him, chuckling to myself. I think I made a friend last night without even knowing it.

"Heyyyyy Batter Batter!" he shouts to me. I try to hide the smile forming, but Cason's humor wins. He'll always win; his goofy personality doesn't allow for anything else.

Cason gets out to push the passenger seat forward for me as I approach the car.

"Uh oh, I don't think Ruth is a morning person either. Maybe I should let you sit in the front with Dickwad here," he says as he points his thumb at Jesse.

"I don't care where the fuck y'all sit, just get in the damn car." Jesse cuts his eyes to us standing outside the car door.

I roll my eyes. Cason laughs and I climb into the back seat next to Jade. The second Cason climbs back into the passenger seat and shuts the door, Jesse throws the car in reverse and peels out of the driveway angrily, taking off down the road.

"I didn't ask for you to pick me up. You don't have to be a caveman, grunting orders and shit all the time."

Jade bursts into laughter and Cason turns his head to look into the backseat, directing a smile at me. "Aw, come on. He sometimes growls too. It's not all grunts. At least, that was the case before you thought you were Babe Ruth and bashed Jax in the head. Big bad Jesse over here thinks you need a bodyguard now."

"Looks like she needs one at home too. This neighborhood is sketchy as fuck. Why would you want to live here?" Jesse mumbles.

My cheeks heat up. I know I don't live in a great neighborhood, but it was the best we could do at the time. "Some of us don't have a rich Daddy to put an AMEX in our pocket." I wrinkle my nose, trying to swallow the bad taste in my mouth.

Jesse glances at me through the rearview mirror just as he puts the car in park in front of a gas station. "Don't kid yourself. That AMEX comes with a price." Jesse climbs out of the car, slamming the door behind him before stalking off.

I have a feeling that anger isn't all about me.

Cason jumps out but pops his head back in. "Y'all need anything. Coffee? Food?"

49

Jade asks for a coffee and a pop tart. Cason turns his head to me. "Ruth?"

I shake my head no, and Cason nods, shutting the door, leaving Jade and me alone. I watch their retreating figures as they both head inside the store.

"He isn't so bad, ya know. He's just so angry. But under all of that anger, he really is a good guy," Jades whispers while staring after her brother in the store. Sadness creeps into her eyes. I don't say anything. Heck, there isn't much I can say. Life isn't always fair, no matter what kind of house you live in. I know that well.

The boys climb back in the car with a drink holder full of coffee and a bag of food. Cason hands a coffee and a Pop-tart back to Jade, then picks up his own coffee and takes a big gulp. I watch Jade blow the steam coming from her cup as Jesse lifts a cup to me. I look up to Cason, and he winks. I look back at the cup, staring at it like it's a snake ready to strike. He watches me and waits. I avert my eyes and grab it from his hand, my mouth already watering over the smell. He faces the steering wheel, puts the car in drive, and pulls out of the parking lot. No one says a word, and I wonder if what Jade said is really true. He just couldn't see past all of his anger.

We pull into the parking lot at school. Jesse backs into a spot in the last row between two SUVs and I sigh in relief when the vehicles block everyone's view of us as we get out. They all gather at the back of the white SUV next to us. I don't follow them or hang around long enough for anyone to notice me. I'm not feeling very sociable towards the crowd that is making my fresh start not so fresh.

But when do I ever feel social?

Before I could get inside, someone calls my name. I look back. Mira's jogging to catch up with me. I keep walking, I don't want to get involved in whatever kind of game she's playing.

"Hey! Fallon! What happened to you Friday night? Jordan said he saw you leaving with Cason Cruise?" She sounds a little winded from her short jog.

"Sounds like you already know what happened," I tell her.

"What do you mean?" she glances at me.

"Look. I don't know what kind of friends you're used to, but I don't bring friends out and spend the whole night sucking face with my boyfriend, ignoring them. Especially not after their friend," I air quote the word friend with my hands, "gets manhandled by some guy that everyone at this school seems to have beef with."

"Wait, What? You had a run-in with Jax?" she asks.

It's funny how she knows who I'm talking about. We reach my locker, and I throw the door open.

"What? Your pretty-boy boyfriend didn't tell you? He was out in the parking lot for the whole show." I grab my books, stuffing them into my bag.

"No, he didn't tell me any of that. He just said you left with Cason, and I thought . . ."

"Nice. He sounds like a real winner." I shut my locker door and turn to her. "You thought what? That I was like you and Narni, going off to sleep with Jesse's bestie? It's called a ride home, Mira. And that's another thing. You were supposed to give me a ride home, and you got drunk. I had to get home somehow."

"Look, I'm sorry. I had a rough afternoon with my parents, and I just needed to let loose. I swear I don't usually act that way," she pleads. "I didn't know what happened. I swear, I would never have drunk so much if I'd known."

I release a sigh. "Fine, whatever. It's cool."

Her face lights up. "Yeah?"

"Yeah. Ok, I get it, but don't leave me hanging like that again. That wasn't cool with me," I say. We walk down the hallway to class together.

Homeroom goes by quickly. I barely pay attention, and my mind keeps wandering. When the bell rings, it startles me out of my daydream. I'm going to have to ask for someone's notes. I wasn't mentally present for that class at all.

I go downstairs so I can switch out my books before next class, and I notice a few people glancing in my direction as I approach my locker. I'm getting used to the looks, but I quickly realize they are staring for a reason today. I stop walking when my locker—and a very visible Jesse—comes into view. He's leaning against the wall next to my locker, waiting. For me.

What. Is. He. Doing?

He looks up and sees me standing there, staring at him. His eyebrows knit together, and his head tilts as he continues to watch me. One of his eyebrows lift. I swallow my shock, forcing myself to walk. I reach my locker and pretend like he's not standing right next to me with everyone's eyes on us.

"Where did you go this morning?" he asks.

"What are you doing?" I hiss, not looking him in the face.

His eyebrows furrow as I try to make myself as small as possible. "I . . ."

"I left. I don't have to be in this little gang you guys have going on. I'm fine on my own," I whisper yell, glancing at him.

A hint of confusion spreads over his face but quickly turns into a frown as realization dawns. "You don't want people to see you with me."

I swallow back a large knot in my throat. Somehow his words make me feel so vulnerable. I peer up at him, his eyes lock on mine. "I don't want people to see me at all."

We stay like this in silence. The air around us is electrifying from, I don't know, understanding, maybe?

I feel an arm loosely wrap around my neck from behind, pulling me into a warm, hard body. Jesse is quiet, watching my discomfort. I squeeze my eyes shut.

This cannot be happening right now.

When I open my eyes, Jesse is still watching me, his frown only growing.

"Ruth! My favorite slugger. What's up?" Cason's voice vibrates through me.

He raises his hand for a fist bump, and Jesse meets it with his own. His eyes never leave mine.

Cason speaks up again, either completely clueless of our exchange or choosing to ignore it. I never know with him.

"You give her the heads up about practice yet?" Cason says. His voice carries, bringing more attention to us. To me.

Jesse clears his throat, appearing uninterested, bringing his mask up.

That's right, keep that wall up. Why let it down for me?

52

"We have a late practice today. I gave my keys to Jade. She'll give you a lift home."

I nod, wanting to argue, but I'm very aware that everyone is now staring at us. Or I should say at me, the new girl now on everyone's radar, thanks to these two. The urge to run away is itching its way down my legs, almost unbearable in its intensity.

Jesse jerks back in surprise when I don't argue, but he quickly disguises it with a sharp nod, marching off without saying another word.

I watch as everyone's eyes follow him down the hall, including mine. He has a purpose in his stride, and his head is always held higher than those around him. I will give it to him—the boy has swagger. That is clearly evident when every girl swoons as he passes.

Cason erupts in laughter, dropping his arm from my shoulders to clench his abdomen, "Oh man, this is gonna be *so* good. You're under his skin, and he has no idea what to do with that."

He walks backward so he can face me as I shut my locker, following him down the hall.

"Ruth, I think you're better at the game than we all thought," he goads with an authentic Cason smirk. He throws me a wink and steps away into the hallway leading down to the right, where his next class must be.

I roll my eyes, never breaking my stride as I walk away with my middle finger in the air. I hear Cason chuckle. I struggle to hide the smile he brings to the surface. It's the one I try so hard to keep away, but man, is he good at finding it.

CHAPTER NINE

By Friday, I have a new routine. It's the same every morning: I wake up, get dressed, and wait for him to honk. All week, Jesse has made sure I had a ride to and from school. We stop for coffee every morning, and Jesse silently hands me a cup. After school, the four of us pile in the car, and he always drops me off first. On practice days, Jade brings me home, after her cheer practice, in Jesse's car. The cheer thing is unexpected, Jade defies everything I thought a cheerleader to be. But who am I to judge, so I do my homework while I wait for her to finish. I enjoy the quiet on these days anyway.

I haven't said a whole lot about my new babysitters. If I was honest, the entire situation makes me a little uncomfortable. Although, when I do huff about it, Jade says it's because they are afraid that Jax might figure out who I am. I argued that fact when Cason and Jade decided I needed to sit with them at lunch, too. When I brought up that my corner was only a few feet away and that not much could happen there, Jade just shrugged her shoulders and said that she likes having another girl in the group. I decided not to argue much after that. I understand what it's like to be surrounded by people but still feel alone. Cason laughed at this. He thinks of Jade as one of the guys. Cason's nickname for me has stuck. Now the entire group is calling me Ruth, except Jesse. He let "New Girl" go and has started calling me by my real name, because Ruth is "so stupid to him." I eye my corner once more, taken aback when I find Mira sitting in her usual spot, watching me. I avert my eyes. I can't help but feel like I'm abandoning her.

"She's not one of us," Jesse says from across the table, eyeing me. Everyone looks up, trying to figure out what Jesse is talking about. I glance back to my corner. Mira is gone, but a box of candy sits in her place. I frown, not sure how to handle it.

On Monday morning, I'm putting all of my books back into my bag when the honk comes. I check the time on my phone; they're a few minutes early. I hurry to zip up my bag and call out to my mom that I'm leaving. When I make it to the car, Cason doesn't step out, as usual, to let me in. I scrunch my eyebrows together and reach for the passenger door. When I open it, Jesse is sitting behind the wheel, alone. I stand there, feeling slightly unsure.

"Are you going to get in?" he asks.

I slowly lower myself into the passenger seat, wary of being in the car alone with Jesse. I place my bag between my legs on the floorboard and glance at him.

"Jade had a breakfast thing for the cheerleading squad, so Cason drove her."

I nod, the awkwardness level meeting a new high. Jesse pulls into the gas station for morning coffee, and my stomach growls, reminding me that I haven't eaten anything for breakfast.

He goes inside the store, and I take the time to breathe. I'm not sure I'm ok with this situation. When he finally reappears, he has two coffees and a black plastic bag hanging from his hand. He hands a cup over to me when he gets back in the car along with the bag he was carrying after grabbing a protein bar out of it. I peek into it and see one lonely blueberry muffin lying on the bottom. I look back to Jesse, but he's already backing out of the parking spot as if this is normal for him.

"What is this?" I ask.

"You didn't have anything with you to eat, and I could hear your stomach growling from over here." He shrugs his shoulders, keeping his eyes on the road.

"I . . ." I frown and look back to the muffin. "Thanks." I give him a small smile before tearing open the wrapper, shoving a huge bite in my mouth. I close my eyes and almost moan when it hits my tongue. I really am starving.

Jesse stays quiet for most of the drive, lost in thought—or so I thought.

"Why is it so hard for you to accept that people can be nice?"

I snap my head in his direction, not expecting that. I consider his question and decide to answer him honestly. "Because I've seen the ugly in this world."

"Who was it? Who broke you?"

"Someone I trusted my everything to."

We arrive at school, but Jesse doesn't pull into his usual spot. He pulls up behind Cason's Jeep, throwing the car into park. I grab my bag, opening the door to get out. But I realize Jesse isn't moving, and I stop.

"Are you not getting out?" I ask him.

"Nah, I think I'm gonna skip today." He gazes up to me with so much seriousness that I immediately know something isn't right with him.

I look at all the kids walking into school. I don't want to be here either, if I'm honest.

I settle back into the passenger seat and close my door. I'm not sure what I'm doing, but I do know one thing. I'm not going into that school today.

"What are you doing?" He raises that pierced eyebrow at me.

"I think I'm skipping too," I tell him.

He looks surprised, but that surprise slowly turns into a soft smirk. He hits the brake and shifts the car into drive. "Last chance to exit this car."

I stay, trying to appear more confident than I actually am. The car starts rolling, causing me to swallow hard.

"Ok, I gave you the chance."

I'm positive that I'm going to regret this later.

We drive for what feels like an hour. Jesse brings us down a gravel road. Tall grass and trees line either side of us. I'm starting to worry that he's going to try to leave me out in the middle of nowhere. I chuckle to myself.

"What's so funny?" he glances at me.

Shit, did I laugh out loud?

"Just imagining you ditching me out here." I laugh again.

"You really think I would leave you out here? I would never. If for no other reason, I would never hear the end of it from Jade and Cason." He laughs too.

He slows the car to a stop in front of a small cut out of the trees. I lean over him to look through his window. A glint of water reflects off the sun.

"Where are we?" I ask him as I sit back.

He nods his head to the door. "Come on. You're about to find out."

I get out of the car, ambling around to the other side. He holds his hand out to me, and I stare at him incredulously.

"I won't bite," he chuckles. "This time."

I grab hold of his hand, letting out a deep breath. He leads me through a cutout in the trees and down a slightly steep hill. As we get closer to the bottom, I realize we are on the bank of Cherry Creek Lake. I let go of his hand, and take a few steps to look out over the water, and my breath hitches. It's a gorgeous view. The water is calm, and the birds are singing. It relaxes my body almost instantly.

"It's pretty cool, huh?" Jesse says.

"It's beautiful," I mumble, lost in the scene.

"That's not even the best part." He grabs my hand again, leading me back up the drop-off, helping me when I lose my footing and begin to slide down. We get to the top, and he drops my hand, running over to a tree that hangs out over the water. He grabs onto the bottom limb, hoisting himself up.

58

Is he really going to climb this tree?

"Jesse, what are you doing? You're going to fall and break something!" I yell up at him. He's already several feet up.

"Chill. It'll be ok," he calls down.

I stand there, staring up at his monkey form. He's so high I can only see his feet dangling. A loud crack sounds out, and I scream. I just know he's falling. I finally talk myself into looking. Instead of his crumpled body at the base of the tree, I see a thick rope hanging down, dragging on the ground. He jumps down, landing on his feet in front of me. He's laughing at me when he straightens. I feel my neck and face warm up as I avoid his eyes.

"What was that noise you made?" he asks with a grin still gracing his face.

"You mean when I screamed? I thought your dumb ass had fallen." I smack him on the shoulder.

"Nope. Wasn't me. See, I'm fully intact." He raises his arms and turns in a circle to make his point.

I roll my eyes when he turns back to face me, but he just gives me one of those smiles that you know for sure means he's about to cause trouble.

"Are you ready?" he asks.

"Ready? For what?" I raise my eyebrow.

He looks to the rope, then back to me.

"What do you want me to do with that?"

His eyes widen at the same time his mouth drops open. "You've never been on a rope swing?"

"You want me to swing from that?" I squeal as I point to the dangling rope.

His laughter rolls over me, warming me all over. I've never heard him laugh this much.

Jesse pulls his shirt over his head and drops his jeans.

"What are you doing?!" I squeak out as I quickly cover my eyes.

"I'm not about to get in the water in my clothes. I left my boxers on. You can open your eyes."

I uncover one eye slightly to make sure his boxers were entirely in place before I drop my other hand. Jesse reaches over the drop off to grab the rope, pulling it back a few feet with him. He tests the line with his weight to make sure it would hold and looks to me to make sure I saw.

"Watch me. It's fun—I promise."

He places his hands together high on the rope and adjusting his grip before leaning back a bit. After one last pause to get situated, he jumps up, grabbing the rope with his feet. He swings out over the water, giving a full-bellied laugh—one that sounds genuine and real. I've never seen him this relaxed and loose before. I'd almost forgotten he's an actual teenager before this moment. When he's far enough out, he releases his grasp on the rope and falls into the water with a huge splash.

He's crazy!

His head pops up, shaking the water out of his face. He looks up, scanning the ledge for me.

"Your turn!"

"No way. Nope," I tell him as I back away from the drop-off.

A slow, lazy smile crosses his face. He swims to the bank, gets out of the water, and climbs all the way up the ledge I'm watching from. When he reaches the top, he stands, stalking over to me. He shakes out his hair, splashing me with cold water.

"That water is freezing!"

"It's only cold for a moment. You get used to it," he says as he pulls the rope back again. This time, he looks at me, waiting.

"Jesse, I can't. I'm sorry, but I would like to keep all the pieces of my body *on* my body." I shake my head to the side.

"What if we do it together?" he holds his hand out to me.

"That rope will not hold both of us."

He chuckles as his hand meets his face, rubbing away a few drops of water.

"This rope is strong, and the tree is sturdy. It'll hold." He holds his hand out again. "Trust me, Fallon. Please?"

I look from his hand to the rope and back again. Then I look up into his pleading eyes. He really wants me to trust him. No, I think he *needs* me to. I scrunch my eyes closed for a long second, knowing I won't say no, not even if I wanted to.

Resigning myself to it, I say, "Fine. Turn around." I'm thankful that I wore a tank top under my shirt this morning. I strip down to just my tank and underwear. I clear my throat, and Jesse turns around. His eyes stop on my legs before he looks back to the rope, averting his eyes.

"Come here," he says a bit gravelly.

I stand in front of him, and he puts his hands on my shoulders, turning me towards the water.

"On three, I want you to jump onto the rope. Grab it with your feet. I'm going to hold on to you with one hand. When we get out over the water, you have to let go. Ok?" His chest is touching my back as his breath rubs across my shoulder. I nod, too afraid to speak. I know if I do, he'll hear how much our current position is affecting me. His hands glide down my forearms and he grabs onto my wrists. I take a deep breath in through my nose, trying to keep the shivers away before he feels them. He places each of my hands onto the rope, one above the other.

"Like this. You have to use your arms to pull you up."

I let out the air from my lungs as I fight the urge to run away.

His arm wraps around my waist, and my nerves heighten.

"One . . . two . . . three!"

I squeal and jump onto the rope. Jesse holds me tight as we fly over the ledge and up towards the sky. It's so quick that I forget to let go.

"Let go now, Fallon," Jesse whispers into my ear. I hold on for a beat longer, feeling a small bit of fear rising up. "You have to let go!"

I hold my breath, loosening my hands and feet. My body becomes weightless for a few short moments as I fall toward the lake. Cold water slams into me and swallows me whole. I kick my feet hard, pushing my way to the surface through the murky lake water. I break the surface of the water and smile at Jesse who appears just a few seconds later near me.

"So?"

My smile only gets fuller.

"Again!" This time I race him to the top.

CHAPTER TEN

It's nearing three o'clock. The school will be letting out soon, and this short vacation from the real world will come to an end. We've been out here for most of the day. We're lying on the bank, drying off in the hot sun.

"Do you come out here a lot?" I ask, glancing at him.

"Yeah, sometimes. I mean, I'm usually alone." His eyes are trained to the water. "It's calm. And quiet. There's no bullshit out here."

He looks to me, but he isn't looking at me. He's someplace else entirely. His body is sitting right next to me, but his mind has drifted off to wherever it goes when he's out here. When I look into his face, he doesn't look angry with his walls up all the way to the clouds. He just looks like Jesse, a boy in high school.

I lean back on my arms but continue to watch. As much as I hate to admit this, I could watch him like this all day.

"I get it. Back at home, I had an elderly neighbor, Mrs. Gladys. She had a beautiful flower garden in her backyard," I begin. "I used to go over there when my mom was working late. I would spend the afternoon out there with her. But sometimes, when it all became too much, I would sneak over there at night and lay on this pretty iron bench that she had right in the middle of all the flowers. I would just lay there staring at the stars, smelling the flowers. It was the same for me. It was quiet and peaceful. My shadows wouldn't follow me there. It was safe."

We continue to watch the water. An understanding weaves through us.

We stay like this for another hour, in the silence of it all, just enjoying the peace. Unfortunately, Jesse eventually stands up and offers me his hand.

"Come on, we have to go." His gruff voice washes over me, pulling me out of my contentment.

I reach for his hand, and he hauls me quickly to my feet. We climb up the ledge to reach our clothes. Jesse puts his on in record time before taking off to his car. Without waiting for me.

 The walls are back.

He waits for me to join him in the car. I quietly get in and shut the door, afraid I might spook this version of Jesse. He hits the gas as soon as the door clicks. I thought we were starting to understand each other today, but it looks like I might've been very wrong.

I assume Jesse is going to take me directly home, but before I know it, we're pulling into the school parking lot.

"What are we doing here?" I ask him.

He just looks at me, as silent as he was during the entire drive here.

Jesse parks in the same spot in the last row. I've learned that no one parks here except Jesse. This spot is off-limits to anyone—unless you want to find your car keyed, or even worse, the tires slashed. I get out, and before I can shut the car door, Jade is on me. She pulls me towards the back of the car where the entire gang, including Jordan, Mira's boyfriend, is hanging out.

"Hi, friend! Why does your hair look like you've been swimming?" I look up at her quickly, then glance to Jesse. "Nevermind, I don't care. Guess what?"

"What?" I say, throwing a little sarcasm into the word.

"The boys have an away game tonight. Do you know what that means?" She has an evil grin spreading across her face, which usually means trouble with her.

"Do I want to know?"

Jade rolls her eyes at me. "Can you at least *try* to pretend you like us and want to have some fun together?"

"Why would I do that? I mean, it's not like your evil twin has a chain wrapped around me, holding me in his shadow. Oh, wait! That's right, he does." I give her the fakest smile I have in me.

Cason barks in laughter. "Ruth got jokes!"

Jesse, who is leaning on the back of his car, cuts his eyes towards Cason and tries to force away the tiniest of smiles.

"Fallon, you know he's just trying to protect you."

I prop myself against the side of Cason's Jeep, which just happens to be where the white SUV is typically, and lift my foot to the tire. "Who are we beating up tonight? Better yet, should I bring a bat this time?"

"Even better. The basketball team is playing against a team in Jennings. It's a few towns over. I have to go with the cheerleading squad. But I'm thinking of getting an extra room at the hotel the school booked for the players. Then we can hit up a club we know that serves minors."

I stare at her like she has two heads.

"No. Nope." I throw my hands up. "I'm not going. No way."

"Come on, Fallon. Don't make me pull the evil twin brother card. You know he'll put you over his shoulder and bring you, willing or not. It will be fun. Besides, I don't want to be the only girl with the guys."

"You won't be the only girl. Cason's hand will be up the shirt of the first girl he sees." I smirk. Cason tries to interject, but I don't let him get a word in. Pointing at him, I say, "Don't even try and say it's not true because you know it is."

He shrugs his shoulders and smiles at me while I shake my head.

"Jesse wasn't at school today. How does he still get to go?" I ask.

Cason snorts. "No way Coach will penalize his best point guard."

"It doesn't matter. You're all forgetting one important thing."

"What?" Jade looks around to everyone.

"I don't have an ID. I can't get into a club."

Jade smiles from ear to ear, and I know I have no shot in hell of getting out of this. When Jade gets an idea in her head, there is no stopping her.

"I have that taken care of."

"Do I even get a choice?" I ask looking at Jesse.

65

He slowly smiles with a tilt of his head. "Sure. Do you wanna sit shotgun, or in the trunk?"

CHAPTER ELEVEN

Jade brings me home since the boys have to meet at the bus they're taking for the game.

Everyone else had already packed an overnight bag, leaving me to go home and pack on the fly. Jade comes in with me "to make sure I pack more than my t-shirt and jeans for the club." She finds a pair of black skinnies and a red tank from the back of my closet that I didn't even know I had. I'm pretty sure my mom put them in there with the hope I would wear them. This is the same mom who, by the way, is so excited that I'm going somewhere at all, that she's helping Jade pack my bags. I stretched the truth a bit, telling my Mom we're going with Jade's parents to the game.

When Jade asks if I have any heels, I look at her with a blank face. My mom runs out of the room and comes back shortly with a pair of black pumps. I groan and throw a pair of jeans and a t-shirt in the bag when neither one of them are looking.

After I'm convinced that I can burn everything in my duffel, I hug my mom goodbye. She smiles at me so brightly that I can't keep from smiling back. It's only because a part of me really wants her to not worry about me. If I have to fake a smile and go along with a crazy idea like this one to make her happy, then I will.

"Dude, your mom is way cool. She didn't even flinch when you told her where you were going and what you were doing. My mom has a built-in lie detector. She would've called me on it before I'd even said a word," Jade says as soon as we get in the car.

"Yeah. She just really wants me to have a normal teenage experience, you know?" I mumble.

"Well, that's really awesome." Jade laughs.

We arrive back at school just in time to see the team loading up on the bus. Jesse comes jogging over to the car, and I roll my window down allowing him to lean in.

"Coach doesn't want any of us driving, so you're going to have to drive my car there. Is that cool?" He asks, looking at his sister. My opinion doesn't matter. I'm going because he says I am.

Jade nods. I stare back and forth. Waiting on at least one of them to acknowledge me.

"Okay, make sure you follow the bus close. I want to be able to see you at all times."

Jade salutes her brother. "Sir, yes, sir!"

Jesse rolls his eyes at his sister and jogs back over to the bus without so much as a glance in my direction. Coach Henry is yelling at him to hurry up. Jesse rolls his shoulders but doesn't say anything as he steps onto the bus.

So, he does know how to listen. Good to know.

It's about a two-hour drive to the opposing team's school. As we pull into the parking lot, I notice a lot of kids from our school hanging out by their cars.

"Did the whole school come?" I ask Jade.

"Ha, just about. If you think they would miss out on getting an unsupervised hotel room and partying with the team, you're crazy. Most of the girls will try to end up in the bed of one of the guys on the team before the night is over."

"The coach doesn't check on them?"

"Nope, he gets a room on a separate floor. He does room checks around ten, and then he doesn't come out of his room till morning."

We enter the school gym, and Jade spots their usual group in the bleachers. We pile next to a few of the girlfriends of some of the players one bleacher up.

The game is exciting. Jesse and Cason play almost like they're dancing, always anticipating each other's moves, just like the night of the fight. Always being where the other needs them. Jesse shot three-pointers all night, making it look easy. The other team is good, but our boys are better.

Our boys?

What is going on with me? They aren't *my* anything but bossy boys whom I can't seem to shake.

"I'm going to get a water. You want anything?" Jade asks.

"No, I'm good."

"Ok, I'll be right back." She climbs down the bleachers and disappears through a side door.

"That didn't take long," Jordan says from behind me.

"I'm sorry?" I twist to face him.

"Callaway. He already has you under his thumb."

"What are you talking about?"

"Jesse. He's controlling you. Like he does the rest of this school." He looks out onto the court with his lip curled up.

"Uh, aren't y'all friends?" I ask.

"Sure." He smiles, but there's a hint of something there that makes me question his answer.

Jade climbs back to the seats, finding her spot again and I turn back to the game. But I can't focus. The way Jordan spoke left me feeling unsettled.

The game finally ends—our team won—and we all go back to the hotel to get ready. Jade and I share a room located right next to Jesse's. I'm sure the fact that we ended up on the same floor as the team, especially knowing the school booked the entire floor, is no coincidence.

As we're getting dressed, the coach goes down the hall knocking on every door right at ten, like Jade said. I knew when I heard shrieks and laughter that he had gone back to his room. I put on the clothes that Jade packed for the club and feel completely out of my element. She insists that I let her do my make-up and curl my hair. I refuse at first. Eventually, I compromise with eyeliner, mascara, a little blush, and lip gloss, and I keep my hair straight and sleek.

She steps back from me as she finishes the last touch.

"Girl, you look *hot*!" She laughs.

A banging on our door startles us both. Cason's yelling voice comes through the door, "You two have got to be done by now. We're ready to goooo."

Oh, Cason.

I open the door to Cason, holding his hand up mid-knock, and Jesse, shaking his head. They both freeze, and I look behind me to figure out what they are staring at.

"What?"

"Damn, Ruth! You look fine!" Cason spins me around before kissing me on the head. He sits on our bed. All the rooms with double beds got booked out by the team, so Jade and I have a king-sized bed to share.

Jesse stands in the threshold with his hands in his pockets, and I take the opportunity to roam my eyes over him appreciatively. He looks good in a loose white shirt layered under a black leather jacket. He must've run some gel through his hair to spike it back a bit. I lift my eyes to his face after I get my feel. He's watching me check him out. We both freeze. There's a force holding us in our own little bubble. We're locked onto each other, and I just can't pull my gaze from his.

Cason picks up a shrieking Jade and throws her over his shoulder.

"Are y'all ready to party?! Let's go!" He carries her out the door screaming, refusing to put her down when she demands it, and I finally divert my eyes, leaving the most intense moment behind.

I grab my phone and cash off of the dresser, stuffing both in my pocket. Jesse holds his hand out, gesturing for me to go first as we walk out of the room. The elevators open just as we reach them. Cason still has Jade over his shoulder, but she's no longer squealing and seems to have given up on getting down. We file into the elevator, and Jesse pushes the button to the first floor. We're standing across from each other, both leaning against the wall. His eyes roam up my legs to my stomach and over my chest until they land on my face. There's a sizzle in his eyes that I can feel from over here. The elevator door opens on the main floor, and Cason is the first one through the sliding doors. Jesse holds my gaze for what feels like hours but is only a few moments more before he slaps his hands onto the edge of the door keeping it from closing, letting me exit first.

It's going to be a long night.

CHAPTER TWELVE

We arrive in an alley that I would consider unsafe if it wasn't for the twenty or so people standing in line. The door to the entrance is open, allowing the pulsating beat of the music from inside to spill out. Jade pulls out two IDs and hands one to me. I chuckle when I look at the Wisconsin driver's license of a girl named Marina Lawson. Looking at her picture, we have the same hair color, but the similarities end there. You can definitely tell it's fake, but the bouncers don't seem to care as long as would-be partiers have something for him to look at.

The club is packed, lights are flashing in every direction, and a large dance floor sits right smack in the center of the building. There is a second-floor balcony, and guessing by the bouncer that is making friends with a red rope, it's reserved for VIPs only.

We decide to hit the bar first. The crowd is so intense that Jesse has to wrap his hand around my waist to keep me from getting lost in the sea of sweaty people. His touch is so soft, but the tension in his arm is purely protective. Jade pulls me by the hand, following Cason's lead. I try to focus on the glow of lights coming from the bar instead of how right it feels to have Jesse's hand there. Cason finds a hole in the throng of people swarming the bartender and orders shots for all of us. As soon as I'm able to touch the bar top, Jesse drops his hand. The loss of his touch makes my body shudder.

The bartender rushes back and forth, preparing drink after shot after drink, leaving us waiting. The guy next to me carries his drinks away, bumping into me in the process. Jesse reaches out and grabs me before I fall face first. While I'm grateful I don't have to touch a floor covered in grime and filth, I'm now in an awkward position. I tense when I realize my hands are splayed across his chest. His large muscles flex underneath my touch. I slowly bring my eyes up to his face. My throat constricts, and I swallow thickly.

The corner of his mouth lifts. "Why are you always falling into me?"

"Why are you always catching me?"

"Who wants shots!" Cason screams over the music and starts passing out shot glasses filled with a clear liquid. I jump back from Jesse and attempt to compose myself, but my heart is hammering in my chest. I take a few deep breaths while I wait for Cason to pick up his shot from the counter.

Cason holds it up for a toast, and we all follow his lead. "To tequila and boobs, women in thongs, and a good ride all night long!"

Cason throws his shot back while we all stare at him, dumbfounded. Jade rolls her eyes at him and taps her shot glass to mine. "Here's to the poor girl who goes home with him tonight."

I chuckle, pouring the warm liquid down my throat. The burn warms my chest. It feels like it's one hundred degrees in here already, but this may just be what I need to deal with this crowd and get through tonight.

Jade grabs me by the arm, yanking me towards the crowded dance floor. "Come on, let's go dance!"

Dancing is something I can do. A remix comes on, and I feel the music flow around me. I close my eyes and just dance, getting lost in the music. The effects of the shot slowly make its way through each limb, relaxing my body enough to make me more fluid. Song after song passes by, causing me to lose time. This is what I needed.

When I finally bring myself out of my music-induced daze, I search the bar area for only one thing. I'm greeted with two smoldering black eyes that follow every sway of my hips. Jesse is leaning against the bar, but when he notices I'm watching him watch me, he stands straighter. His jaw visibly locks down, and I simply observe as he fights the urge to join me. *Why?* I close my eyes again, taking comfort in knowing his eyes are only on me.

The smell of sweat mixed with alcohol hits my nostrils and rough hands grab onto my hips. The touch is all wrong, and panic instantly rises up like vomit as I open my eyes to see the owner of the callouses. I jerk forward, spinning out of the hands of a man who looks to be in his mid-twenties. He sways to the music sloppily, and a glistening sheen on every part of his exposed skin makes him even more off-putting.

"Come on, baby. I just wanna dance," he slurs. My heart may beat right out of my chest if he comes any closer to me. He reaches out for me again, grabbing hold of my wrist as I yank back, desperate to put any amount of distance between us. I push and kick until I double over, unable to breathe through the panic. I gulp in air as my entire body trembles. The sounds around me are distorted. I try to focus on breathing in and out. An ache forms quickly through my chest, making me grab onto my heart. I swear I can feel myself dying as my world spins on its axis. My tears begin to fall faster, soaking through my pants and leaving a warm trail down my thigh.

A soft hand touches my face, and relief falls over me. This touch feels right, safe. A blurry version of Jesse's face comes into focus when I pry my eyes open.

"Fallon. Look at me, you're okay. You have to breathe slower for me. You're hyperventilating."

He winces as he grips the back of my head, pushing it between my legs. I suck in deep breaths, focused on slowing my erratic heartbeat.

"I'm going to pick you up, okay?"

Speaking is out of the question, so I nod my head.

He wraps my arms around his neck and lifts me with my legs draped over his arm. I hide my face in the crook of his neck. My eyes are squeezed tightly shut. He carries me out of the club doors and straight into a taxi that I'm almost positive someone else called. Jesse leans back into the seat and readjusts me, turning me into him. He places my legs on either side of his thighs, pulling me tight against his chest. I gulp in deep breaths of light sweat mixed with his cologne, as my body continues to shake uncontrollably.

Jesse cradles me to his chest once more when we arrive at the hotel. He carries me to his room, kicking the hotel room door open with me still in his arms. He turns so he can cross the threshold and enter the room without setting me down, and deposits me on his bed. He removes my shoes and throws them to the floor before softly telling me to lie down and stepping away, leaving me to curl up in a fetal position. My breathing is still heavy, but my heart rate is slowing with every passing moment. Jesse comes to the side of the bed with a large t-shirt in his hand. He bends down so we're eye level and pushes the shirt into my hands.

"I thought you might want to change into something more comfortable. I can't get into your room right now, but you can borrow my shirt."

Speaking still feels too difficult for me, so I nod, bringing the shirt to my chest. He gives me his back to allow me to change, but even that task is too difficult for me. I'm able to break out of my tank top and into the shirt, but when I stand up to unbutton my pants, my hands tremble too much to grasp the button. I struggle with it a few times before Jesse brings his hand to mine, stopping me. He looks to me for approval, and after receiving another nod from me, he pulls the button undone. With his eyes still staring into mine, he reaches for the zipper next and slowly drags it down until it stops. I push the waistband of my pants down and step out of my jeans before kicking them into the corner. I keep my eyes locked on his. Jesse reaches for my hand and guides me to his side so he can lean over the bed and pull the covers back. I slowly climb into the bed as he pulls the sheets up and over my body. After he tucks me in, he turns to leave. I quickly reach for his hand, stopping him from walking away.

"Stay. Please," I whisper.

Jesse hesitates for a long minute before turning back. He lifts his shirt over his head and kicks his shoes off. I feel the roughness of his jeans rub against my legs when he slides in close behind me. He brings a hand up and begins to comb his fingers through my hair. The repetitive motion calms me enough to ease my heavy breathing and relax my pulse. I think my mind registers the warm and safe cocoon Jesse's body provides, allowing me to succumb to the exhaustion of the night.

The light flutters through the window, waking me to a pounding in my skull. I roll over and find the covers pulled back where Jesse slept last night. There is a key card lying where Jesse should be. But no Jesse. I sit up looking around the room. It's as empty as the spot next to me. A desolate feeling spreads through me, leaving me with an uneasiness that I can't shake away. I do what I do best when I don't know how to process certain emotions: I push it into my box full of life's troubles and lock it away tight. I get out of bed and return to my room using the key card left for me. A very hungover Jade is lying across the bed sideways, still in last night's clothes.

"What happened to you?" I ask.

"Cason happened. That boy is the devil," she groans. "You feeling better?"

"Huh?" I sit on the edge of my bed and fall to my back.

"Your head? Jesse texted Cason that your head was hurting, and he was taking you back to the hotel."

"Oh, yeah, it's much better."

Why didn't he tell them what happened?

"We need to start packing. The team's going to be leaving soon."

Jade groans again, and I think I hear a few curse words. She rolls over and lifts her head slightly off the bed.

"Is that Jesse's shirt?"

Crap! I forgot I slept in his shirt last night.

"Uh, oh yeah. You had the key card, so I had to stay in the boys' room. Jesse let me borrow it to sleep in."

"Oh man, I forgot all about the key. I'm sorry. Why didn't you call me?"

"You were having fun. I didn't want to take you away from that."

Because I was dying on the inside while your brother caught me yet again.

"Come on, get up. We have to get moving." I throw one of my pillows in her direction.

She groans. "Okay, okay. I'm getting up."

It takes another hour to get Jade up and moving. I end up packing both of our bags and drag them out of the hotel room into the parking lot alone. We finish loading the car just in time for Jesse and Cason to meet us. The coach is allowing them to drive home as a reward for playing a good game. This works out great for Jade, because she can sleep the entire ride home. We pile in, each of us in our usual spots, and Jade falls asleep almost instantly. Cason passes the time scrolling through his phone, and I mostly stare out the window. But I catch Jesse frequently glancing back at me through his rearview mirror. I try to ignore his looks the best I can. I don't feel like talking about it yet, but I know I can't avoid him forever.

He drops Cason and Jade off at their house. Apparently, Cason lives with them, too. I say goodbye to them and move up to the front seat so Jesse can bring me home. It's an awkward silence at first, neither of us really sure of what to say. But I guess that silence eventually becomes too much for him.

"How long have you had panic attacks?" His whisper-like voice burns into me. He seems afraid to ask me. Or maybe he is scared to know what my answer might be.

"About a year." I shift in my seat, completely uncomfortable talking about this.

"He grabbed you. That's why you panicked?" Jesse clenches the steering wheel so tightly that his knuckles start turning a shade of white.

"Yes."

"Were you . . ." He swallows hard. "Have you been . . . ?"

"I wasn't raped, if that's what you're asking."

He loosens his grip on the steering wheel and breathes out a heavy sigh.

"Okay."

He pulls into my driveway, turning off his car, and turns to me warily. He's looking at me like everyone else who has ever seen this side of me does. Like I have a switch that could be flipped at any time. This is why I avoid people: so I don't have to explain why my hands tremble all the time or why crowds make my breathing erratic. I don't want people to see how damaged I am.

But Jesse? I think he is just as damaged as me. It was only a matter of time before he recognized it in me too. I wasn't ever going to be able to hide my pain from him. My pain is the same as his pain.

CHAPTER THIRTEEN

"Y'all game for Pete's? I want pizza." Cason rubs his belly. "I'm starving."

I swear, Cason is always hungry. He must have a tapeworm in there. The boy eats like a horse.

"I could go for some pizza," I say as I meet Jesse's stare in the rearview.

"Pizza it is," he says. He puts the car into gear and takes off in the direction of Pete's Pizza Shack, the towns preferred pizza place.

Less than 15 minutes later, we're seated around the table with hot slices of mouth-watering pizza spread across the table.

"So, let's talk The Bonfire." Jade perks up after swallowing the first bite of a greasy slice of anchovy pizza.

"What bonfire?" I ask.

"Not *what* bonfire. *The* Bonfire. It's in a couple weeks. We usually go," Jade corrects me, excitement gleaming from her eyes.

"It's basically a huge excuse to party. Everyone camps out around a large bonfire by a lake for the weekend," Jesse tells me from across the booth.

"It's a senior tradition. People rent cabins or sleep in tents, and they bring boats to go skiing or wakeboarding. It's so much fun." Jade bounces in her seat. I don't think I've ever seen her this excited.

"It's also a great way to get laid," Cason adds.

"Well, I'm ready to spend the weekend at the lake with y'all." Jade jumps a bit in her seat as she smiles widely at me.

"Y'all? Woah, hold on. Who said I was going?" I throw my hands up. "Just 'cause you and Cason here drink like a fish and like to party doesn't mean I do!"

"Hey, now! I resent that statement. I go for the girls, too!" Cason laughs out.

"I told y'all she wouldn't be down for it." Jesse shakes his head.

"Come on, Fallon. It's fun." She lifts her hands up like she was praying and juts her bottom lip out, giving me her saddest puppy-dog eyes. "Pleaseeee?"

I roll my eyes. "Fine. But I'm not rescuing you from any guy's tent. Same for you, Cason."

"Ah, come on. I don't want to hear that shit about my sister," Jesse grimaces.

"Up for some arcade time?" Cason asks Jade.

"Bet I beat your top score!" Jade hops out of the booth, hightailing it to the arcade that Pete's has in the back with all the classics.

"Did she just . . .? Oh, no. She is about to go *down*." Cason jumps up and chases after Jade. They act like true siblings.

"You're not fine with it," Jesse says. My attention turns to him.

"It doesn't matter, it's all a part of life. I can't stop living because the shadows of my past haunt me," I say somewhat bitterly. Feeling feisty, I continue. "Besides, you're one to talk."

"Me? What does that mean?" he asks, clearly taken aback.

"The situation with your dad. I mean, he might be a dick, I don't know, but that isn't what makes you so angry with him."

Jesse considers my words as I watch. I see through him just as much as he does me. I think that might be what scares me the most about him.

"You're right, it's not. I'm angry because he wants me to be him. He's been grooming me for it since birth."

"And you don't want to be him."

"I'm only eighteen. I don't really know what I want to be. I just know right now, at this moment, I want to be a good friend, brother, and maybe be worth something to someone."

"You already are," I say.

"Are what?" He asks with a tilt of his head.

"All of it. A good friend and brother . . ." I say as I look down to where I am picking at a string coming loose in a hole of my jeans, "and you're worth something to someone. To all of us. To me."

I look up and see his black eyes burning a hole in me. His jaw flexes as he leans forward. His hands, which have been draped across the table, inch just a little closer.

"But I don't matter to him. Not unless I'm useful to him for his precious company," he sneers. "He'll bribe me with anything. Cars. Tracks. Whatever it takes. But he only has one agenda: an heir to the throne."

"Have you ever considered taking his offer and turning it into something you actually do want?"

"What? You mean be his little bitch?" I can hear the defensiveness in his tone, and I know I need to change the tone of the conversation before he shuts down on me completely.

"Not at all. I mean, take the resources that come with the job and do something you love with it. Turn the bad into good," I say.

He leans back into his seat, looking almost stunned. "Huh. I never thought of it that way."

I lift the side of my mouth in a smirk as Jade drops down into the booth next to me. The frown she's wearing tells me she lost to Cason.

"Cason beat you again, didn't he?" Jesse asks.

"Whatever. He cheated," she huffs. She crosses her arms, and a big frown settles across her face.

Cason comes back to the booth with a big smile and holds his hand out to Jesse. Jesse reaches into his pocket, pulls out a twenty-dollar bill, and hands it over to Cason.

"I told you she would pout." Cason laughs as he points at Jade.

"You bet against Jade pouting when she lost? That was dumb," I say to Jesse.

"Cason said he would go easy on her," Jesse grumbles.

"And you fell for that?" Cason snorts.

"Whatever, man. Let's go." Jesse throws some cash on the table and slides out of the booth.

We gather up our things, and when I go to follow Cason and Jade to the door, Jesse grabs my hand, holding me back. "Hey, what you said just now about making it better. Do you really think I could do that?"

"Jesse, I think you could do anything you wanted. You're a leader and it shows, even with them." I nod my head to Cason and Jade. Cason is terrorizing Jade as usual.

Jesse looks to his siblings. I can tell he considers Cason as a brother and never a cousin. A resolve forms on his face before he leads me out of the restaurant with a grip on my hand like I'm the only thing holding him together.

CHAPTER FOURTEEN

All anyone has talked about this week is the upcoming bonfire. I've listened to ramblings about lower classmen making plans to crash the weekend. Little do they know that any freshman who shows up will be crucified by the seniors. There are only a few juniors that are popular enough to participate. Apparently, the Callaways didn't count when they were freshmen and sophomores since they own this town. Now that they're seniors, this year is supposed to be the year to be there.

We get out of sixth period early for a pep rally. The basketball team has a big game tonight. I'm supposed to meet Jade at the entrance to the gym, but she has yet to show.

"What are you doing? You look weird just standing here." Mira's voice distracts me from my thoughts.

"I'm waiting for Jade."

"Of course you are. You seem to be enjoying the inside," Mira says while rolling her eyes.

"Mira, do you have a problem? 'Cause if you do, just say it." I push off the wall to face her.

"Wow. Still pushing everyone away." She yanks the gym door open. "You know, we were friends at one point. It would be nice if you remembered that."

With that, she disappears into the gym.

What the hell was that all about?

"What was that?" Jade asks, gesturing towards a disappearing Mira as she finally walks up to me.

"Nothing. She was just saying hi. Where have you been? I've been waiting."

"That looked like an awkward hello." She snorts. "Sorry I was a little late. Adam stopped me to ask if I'm going to The Bonfire." I'm convinced the squeal she lets out is actually an attempt to burst my eardrum.

"That's good, right?" I ask.

"I'm *so* not going to answer that. You will not ruin this feeling." She reaches for the handle to the gym door, pulling it open. "Let's get inside before all the good seats are gone."

We sit in the second row with the seniors. The JV cheer squad comes rushing out and immediately launch into a series of flips across the court. Their shouts and cheers echo throughout the gym.

I turn to Jade, curious. "Why aren't y'all out there for the pep rally?"

"Senior week. They give the seniors the week off so we can enjoy the game like everyone else," she explains.

The cheerleaders make two lines around the locker room doors, shaking their pom-poms above their heads. They cheer loudly and take a moment to get the crowd amped up before the basketball team runs out of the locker room onto the court. The guys do a few drills for show, but they're having fun with it. Jesse sets his shot up before faking and passing to Cason for an assist.

I watch Jesse as he runs the length of the court. He moves with such ease and looks free—happy, even. He doesn't seem torn down by his father's decision. He just looks like a boy playing a game instead of a man with the weight of the world on his broad shoulders.

"You might want to wipe the drool on your face." Jade bumps her shoulder into mine.

"What?" I snap my head up to her.

"I mean, I know the team is full of hot guys, but you weren't even blinking," she laughs.

I don't want to tell her that it's her pain-in-the-ass brother I'm currently drooling over.

"Oh yeah, they should do a calendar of the team," I joke.

Jade looks at me with an impressed look on her face. "You know, that's not a bad idea. We could do it as a fundraiser to get new uniforms!"

I look at her and I'm positive I see two heads. She's already texting her cheer friends about the calendar.

That's what I get for trying to distract.

The coach comes out and says a few words, then introduces the senior boys on the team. The cheer squad does a dance that I'm pretty sure isn't even close to appropriate for school.

Most of the student body lingers when the pep rally is finally over. The game starts in an hour, and I guess no one sees the point in leaving. Jesse and Cason sit with us for a while. Jade whines about cabins, while Cason argues that roughing it in a tent would be fun. I have a feeling Cason isn't going to win that argument. There's no way Jade is going to sleep in a tent on the ground.

"Hey Jesse, are you starting tonight?" We all look up at the voice. Elizabeth is standing on the court in front of us with her posse behind her.

"Of course he's starting," Cason says.

"Oh well, have a good game, Jess." Her slimy voice irks me so hard, and the wink she just gave Jesse makes me want to vomit. We all watch as she saunters off, giving her ass an extra sway.

"Yes, have a good game, *Jess*," Jade says mockingly.

"Chill. I'm not into her. You know that," Jesse says.

"Does she know that, dude? Because her ass is calling your name," Cason laughs.

"Whatever, man. Let's go before Coach makes us do sprints for being late." Jesse slaps Cason's shoulder and both boys stand up.

"We'll meet y'all at my car after the game," Jesse yells over his shoulder as he jogs towards the locker room.

Jade's eyes are trained across the room where Elizabeth is talking to a guy with a jersey on. But it's the wrong color. It must be a player on the other team.

"I can't stand that girl. She's manipulative and fake," Jade snarls.

Jade rarely gets mad, but when she does, it scares me. It's not the Jade I know.

"Whatever you're thinking, stop. Jesse will be pissed. Let him handle it," I say.

She watches Elizabeth a little longer, and when I look, she's hugging that guy. She finally pulls away, allowing him to jog off through the same locker room doors as our guys.

"Stop worrying about her, and enjoy the game," I urge again. Knowing Jade, she's not going to let it go, but I feel like I have to try to knock some sense into her.

Jade chills out about midway through the game. It's a close one, but a free throw put us in the lead. We win by three points, leaving our team undefeated.

At my old school, I cheered at football games. I'm still learning about basketball, but Jesse and Cason make it easy to enjoy.

Our school ran out onto the court at the buzzer to celebrate, meaning we had to force our way through a large crowd to get to the car. Jesse and Cason come out a side door ten minutes later ready to roll. Jade convinces me to stay the night with her, and Jesse drops by my house so I can grab an overnight bag.

I leave Cason and Jesse in my living room with my mom, while Jade and I quickly pack. When we come out of my room, Cason looks like he's seen a ghost, and Jesse seems uncharacteristically uncomfortable. Both boys shoot out of their seats without so much as a word when I ask if they are ready to go.

I chuckle as they run out the door and turn back to my mom. "What did you do to them?"

She chuckles. "Oh nothing. Have a great night. I love you."

My mom kisses my forehead, and Jade and I walk out the door to join the scared little boys outside in the car.

CHAPTER FIFTEEN

It turns out that The Bonfire is just a great excuse to get drunk for two straight days. I think the entire school is here. I even spot a few freshmen slinking around. Jade rented two cabins; one for us, and one for the guys. Jesse and Cason are still harping about sleeping in tents, but Jade vetoed that before they could pull the tents out of storage. I didn't care either way. I'm more concerned about my swimwear situation.

"You look great. You have amazing curves, and it's about time you show them off." Jade winks at me. I look back in the mirror to examine the yellow bikini I'm wearing. She convinced me to buy it before the trip, but seeing it now, I feel super uncomfortable. It shows more than I thought it would when it was on the hanger. I grab a pair of shorts—against Jade's protests—to give me the illusion of coverage.

"I can't believe I let you talk me into this," I say as I pull my shorts on in quick, forceful movements.

"Girl, you're going to be the hottest one out there." Her grin looks sneaky in a smartass kind of way, like she knows something I don't.

"Let's go. The guys are waiting." I pull my bag over my shoulder and walk out of the cabin before I can completely change my mind.

"Well, well, what do we have here?" Cason walks up in swim trunks and a shirt with cut off sleeves. He's showing off his muscles for the ladies. At least, that's what he keeps telling Jesse. He grabs my hand and spins me around, giving me a once over.

"Dang, Ruth, who knew you had all of that hiding under there?" he says, which earns him a laugh.

"Cason, don't you have a hole to fall in somewhere?" I ask. Cason's ridiculousness is always on show.

"Oh, I definitely do. *That's why I need my slow ass cousin to hurry the hell up*," Cason yells towards the open cabin door.

"Shove it, Cason!" I hear Jade yell. Cason chuckles. He loves to ruffle her feathers. I shake my head as Cason runs into the cabin, making Jade scream. I can't help but laugh at him again.

"It's good to hear you laugh." I hear his deep voice whisper in my ear. His hand grazes my shoulder as my hair is brushed away. I'm not sure if it was the cool air or his touch, but a shiver slinks through my spine all the way down to my toes until I'm a ball of nerves that I don't understand.

The feel of him being so close draws me in, making me tilt my head slightly to allow him better access. His hands find my hips with a firm grip, and he leans down until his forehead presses into the crook of my neck. His grip becomes tighter, leaving his mark.

"What are you doing to me, Fallon?" Jesse's voice is quiet and gravelly. My body leans closer into him as his voice pulls at me.

"Cason, can't you go away? You're like an annoying little kid, always whining." Jade's voice is like a bucket of cold water being poured over my head. Jesse jumps back as I quickly straighten. The remnants of his touch leave me shaken and even more confused about my feelings towards him. Is this lust?

"Jade, there are women in bikinis. *Bikinis*. Down there. You are taking away from my precious time with them."

Jade walks by me with a huff, and I look to Jesse as he shrugs his shoulders with a laugh. Listening to them fight like siblings makes for a long day. With a shake of my head, I follow them down the path to the lake.

We lay out on a sandy area that is supposed to give a beachy vibe until Jesse and Cason pull us onto their friends' boat to go tubing. We stay on the water until it gets dark and it's time for the big bonfire. The fire is already roaring when we dock the boat. The music is blaring, and everyone looks to be having a good time.

"Here, take one." Jade hands me a solo cup filled to the brim with a blue liquid. I take a sip. It's actually not bad, so I take another.

"Be careful with that. Jade is known for mixing drinks that will catch up to you quick," Jesse warns. He sits down next to me and his hand grazes my arm. The zing from earlier reappears. It's enough to make me want to down this entire cup.

I chuckle. "Warning is acknowledged."

We sit in a comfortable silence as we watch the fire together. Between the alcohol and steady roar of the fire, I'm lulled into feeling calm, and I yawn.

"This won't end. They'll be out here the entire night," Jesse murmurs. I'm not even sure if he's really talking to me, but I answer all the same.

"Yeah, I think I'm about ready to call it. I'm pretty tired." I toss the remaining blue liquid in the fire and the flames surge. Jesse and I glance at each other wide eyed. I don't think I want to know what was in my drink.

"I'm burnt myself. I'll walk you back to the cabins." Jesse grabs my hand and leads us away from the party. We continue to walk down the path with our hands linked. He doesn't let go when we get out of view of the party, and I'm not ready to let go when the cabins come into view. The comfort of holding his hand while in a strange place makes me feel safe. I know once I go into my cabin that feeling will be lost, and I'll be back to fighting the mark my shadows have left. A sigh slips past my lips before I'm able to swallow it.

"What's wrong?" Jesse asks, pushing my hair back from my face with his free hand. I peek up at him before turning my gaze to the cabins. I contemplate if I should tell him I won't be able to sleep, but he knows me better than I thought.

"You won't be able to sleep here, will you?"

"I can't . . . I don't sleep well alone."

"Come on." Jesse pulls me towards my cabin. We're nearly to the door before I realize what he's doing, and I try to protest.

"What do you think you're doing?" I ask, barely able to get the words out.

"Going to bed," he says over his shoulder, walking through the door.

"What about Jade? Cason?"

"I'm positive Cason is going to bring some chick back to the cabin, so I wouldn't get much sleep over there anyway. As far as my sister goes, well, I love her and all, but she doesn't get to tell me what I can do." He smirks at me.

"But I . . ."

"Fallon, it's just sleeping." He stands in front of me and lifts my chin with his knuckle until I meet his gaze. His hand skims across my jaw to tuck a piece of hair behind my ear. "If I can help, let me. Please?" He asks softly, calmly, but his eyes are pleading with me.

With a hard swallow, I consent with a dip of my chin. I leave him in the room alone as I change into sleep clothes in the bathroom. I make sure my teeth are brushed before I return.

Jesse is sitting on the edge of the bed shirtless when I come out. He looks up at the sound of the door opening. I walk out in my t-shirt and sleep shorts. His eyes slide up my bare legs and I curse myself for picking these for tonight.

I sit on the bed and bring my knees to my chest. I stare at his back, watching the ridges flex as he moves. I didn't think about how awkward this would be until now.

He twists to look at me and clears his throat, "Um, do you mind if I sleep in my boxers?"

I nod, moving my chin against my knee, the words not forming on my tongue over the nerves flowing through me. It's not like we haven't done this before, but it feels different this time.

I lay down once he's in the bathroom and face away from him. The lights turn off, and not long after, the bed dips behind me. He moves around, and just as I think he's settled, his hands wrap around my waist. I close my eyes as I let him pull me back against his chest. My body molds against his. Every inch of me that's touching him is tingling. My body tries to convince me that this is ok, that it means nothing. My mind disagrees. Too bad my mind never wins.

Jesse's warm breath grazes my shoulder as he pulls me tighter.

"Jesse, can I ask you a question?" I ask.

"Yes."

I turn in his arms to face him, wrapping my arm around his waist.

"What did Jade mean by it was your fault I was there at the party?"

He squirms at first, considering my question carefully. I think I see fear as the storm in his eyes dilates. I begin to worry as I wait for his answer. Finally, he sighs.

"You've got to understand. They'd all do anything to be us. They'd manipulate and lie to your face. That school is ruthless. But you came along and wanted nothing to do with anyone. It made me curious. So, I sent Jade over there to ask you to come to the party. I wanted to figure you out."

"You could've just asked me, you know?" I whisper.

"I didn't think you would go. And I wanted you to," he says.

With our arms and legs in a tangled heap he kisses the top of my head and says, "Go to sleep Fallon."

And I do. I sleep soundlessly.

CHAPTER SIXTEEN

Jade and I are back on the beach in the sun, watching the boys play volleyball. With my shades on, because I have been appreciating the view.

"*Oh*, look at him. He's *fine*. I might have to see about that tonight at the crawfish boil." Jade pulls her sunglasses down to the tip of her nose to eye a guy who is joining the volleyball game.

I laugh. "He's alright."

She rolls her eyes. "He's alright, or he isn't Jesse?"

I cut my eyes to her, but thankfully she can't see behind my big sunglasses. "What are you talking about?"

"Don't think I didn't notice my brother in your bed last night when I got back," she remarks, pushing her glasses back in place.

"We were just sleeping. He knew I wouldn't be able to sleep and was just trying to help." I don't sound convincing, even to myself.

Jade laughs at me. "If that's what you call it. Let me know when y'all aren't in denial about what's going on between you two. It's so obvious—y'all have that crack and sizzle."

I don't know what to say. I'm not sure she's wrong. The thought has me so deep in my head that I don't notice the unwanted visitor blocking my view of the game.

"I see they let the trash come out." I know that voice, and I could never forget that whine. Elizabeth Creightor in the flesh.

I turn to Jade. "Oh look, they let the princess down from her tower," I say. But Jade's eyes are focused on Elizabeth.

Elizabeth rolls her eyes. "Why don't you keep your trash to yourself and stay out of my way. Jesse is mine. Well, he was going to be before you showed up."

I sit up at this, pushing my sunglasses on top of my head so she can see the seriousness in my eyes. "Let me explain something to you. You might like to play childish games to try get the attention of a boy that doesn't even notice you, but I do not. So if you want to come over here and try to intimidate me, it won't work." I stand and step right in her space. "If Jesse wanted you, he would have you. That's how he works. The fact that you're begging for his attention tells me not only that he doesn't want you, but he doesn't even *see* you."

I can almost see the steam wafting out of her ears and the horns growing on her head.

"Watch it, New Girl. I've been playing this game a lot longer than you have. I'll get what I want. I always do."

I laugh and look over at Jesse, who has stopped playing to watch our exchange. She needs a reality check, and I'm going to give it to her.

"You didn't know? New Girl is so last year. So are you and Jesse." I made sure to add a little whine in my voice, just for her.

I strut to Jesse, who's watching me warily. When I'm within an arm's reach, I grab the back of his neck and pull him to me. I stand on my toes and tip my face towards his. He brings his lips down to greet mine as his hands instinctively find my hips. I touch my tongue to his lips asking for access, and he grants it to me. I groan into the kiss as it deepens, and his hands tighten. Something like desire is growing in me, wanting more from him, and more is what he gives me. He pulls me into him, closing any remaining space between us, his hands sliding up my ribcage, over my breasts, until he's caging my face in his hands. I've never experienced a kiss on this level. It's intense and rugged. It's like my insides are on fire; it's almost too much. I'm afraid he'll burn me. I yank back. Both of us are breathing heavy and the shock I feel is written across Jesse's face. I've forgotten the purpose of coming over here.

"What was that?" he whispers. I sober when I realize nothing about that kiss was real, not even the tingling of my lips. I turn towards the spot I left Elizabeth in.

"Solving my problems." I watch her storm off, but it doesn't give me any satisfaction. Maybe because I know I've only complicated things further without meaning to.

I begin to walk away, the urge to get away from the disaster I just created growing with each passing second, but Jesse catches my arm, keeping me rooted in my spot. He leaves me with only one option, and I look up at him when he steps into my line of sight. The desire that was present a few moments ago is gone. In its place is anger—and it is fierce.

"If you want to kiss me, I won't stop you. But don't *ever* use me like that again. I'm not here for your convenience." His growl makes me wince. That's precisely what I did. I used him to make her go away.

I nod, the knot in my throat stopping me from speaking. This time he lets me go when I pull away, and I run all the way back to the cabin.

After several minutes of arguing with Jade about my clothes, she finally gives up on putting me in a dress tonight. I let her convince me to leave the cabin, but my clothes are non-negotiable.

"We're going to eat crawfish. It's messy, and I don't want to ruin good clothes," I say. She hates it when I wear a t-shirt and jeans with my Converse.

She rolls her eyes. "Come on. I told the guys we would meet them over there half an hour ago."

"Oh, they aren't walking with us?" I ask, disappointment reigns over me.

She sighs. "Nah, Cason said something about a girl. I don't know. But I told them we would meet them over there when we were done getting ready."

She grabs her purse and avoids looking me in the eye, but that's okay—I didn't want her to see the disappointment on my face anyway.

95

I didn't want to feel the frustration that accompanied it, either. It didn't make sense to me. Jesse just sees me as his problem to fix, but somewhere along the way, my feelings seem to have forgotten that.

We walk over to the fire pit where the bonfire was last night. Instead of a massive mountain of wood lit up like an S.O.S. signal, there are tables covered in newspaper and a strong spice filling the air. It's unfamiliar to me, but it meant the crawfish boil had started. Jesse and Cason are already here, each with a beer in hand. Jesse avoids my gaze while he talks to some of his buddies. That kiss has changed something between us, and I'm not sure how to handle it. I will him to look at me as I stare in his direction, but he doesn't. A part of me, a more confident part that I never let out, wants to march up to him and demand that he talk to me. Another part, an unsure part that is always hovering around the surface, wants to go back to the cabin and avoid it all.

"Here, this'll help." Jade hands me one of her famous blue drinks. And I figure, why not? It's not like I have anything to lose. I take a big gulp of it, hoping it helps me forget. Even if it's only for a few hours.

The crawfish are thrown onto the tables pot by pot. The music seems to grow in volume as the night goes on. By the time I eat, they've mixed so much seasoning with them they are unbearably spicy. It's not something we have often here in Cherry Creek, but apparently, one of the senior girls has family in the south that is willing to ship them to us.

I've never eaten crawfish before, and by the time I learn how to peel them, I'm covered in the red juice and my lips are burning. After struggling for a while, I give up on filling up. I go to the bathhouse to clean up. I reach the outside sinks and before I can turn the water on, something barrels into me, almost causing my ass to eat grass.

"Oof. Oh, sorry. I didn't see you there," a male voice says. I peer up at my attacker and am blinded by blonde hair and pearly white teeth. But even through all that, I recognize him as the player that Elizabeth was handsy with at the game this past week.

"Please, you go." He motions to the sink.

"Oh, thanks. Sorry," I mumble as I jump into motion. I wash my hands as quickly as possible. I can feel his stare on me, and it's bringing my comfort level way down. I glance over my shoulder a few times to see him eyeing me closely. I didn't realize that washing your hands could be this entertaining.

I step away to dry my hands. "All yours."

I give a polite smile and throw my trash in the nearest trash can, leaving the awkward moment behind me—or so I thought. I head towards Jade, who's at the drink table again, but the same voice catches up to me, making my escape impossible.

"Hey, wait up." I glance over my shoulder but don't slow down. I can feel my nerves kicking in at being approached by a strange boy, and I want to run.

He matches my stride, obviously not going away.

"Hi, I'm Stephen." He steps in front of me and holds his hand out, forcing me to stop walking. I glance down at his hand, still extended towards me with a frown. "It's just a handshake. Do they not do that where you're from?"

I slip my hand into his with some hesitation.

"Hi, Stephen."

I pull out of his lingering hold and fold my arms across my chest in front of me.

"Hi. So, what's your name?" he asks, his damn smile only getting brighter as he cocks his head to the side.

"Not really into sharing," I say.

"Okay, No-Name. Are you from the Cherry Creek or Westminster Public?"

I look around and scrunch my nose. "Public is here?"

"Oh, don't sound so disturbed. We aren't all bad."

"Oh no, it's not that. It's just this is a Cherry Creek Senior party. I didn't think Public was invited."

"Some of us were. My cousin invited me." He winks.

I finally pause for a moment, and take him in. Looking him up and down, he's got a tall frame, relaxed, broad shoulders, a warm smile, nice clothes, and an expensive watch. The public schools here aren't known for their wealth, but he doesn't seem to fit that crowd. I should probably relax, not every man who approaches me is going to be a bad person.

"It's Fallon. Fallon Blake," I say quickly before I regret it.

"Ah, so the pretty girl does have a name. Tell me, does she also have a boyfriend?" His irresistible charm is starting to brighten my mood.

I give a weak laugh. "No, this girl doesn't have a boyfriend."

"Good. That's good." His smile turns up a few watts. "Well, Fallon, I know this is kind of weird since you don't really know me yet, but would you like to go on a boat ride? We're all going out on the water to watch the sunset."

I look towards the glistening water where a boat pulling up to the dock.

"Uh, maybe. Do you mind if I bring a friend though? Just one more?" I ask. I'm hoping he says yes, because there is no way I'm getting on that boat alone.

"Yeah, sure. I think we could fit one more."

"Cool, I'll go get her and meet you over there." Pointing towards the docks, I ask, "It's the boat that just pulled up to the dock, right?"

"Yeah, that's it. I'll meet you there."

"Sure, okay. Meet you there," I say. A slight smile makes its way onto my lips as I walk in search of Jade.

It doesn't take much convincing when I tell Jade that a guy named Stephen asked if we would like to see the sunset on his boat.

"Stephen Rogers? *Westminster Public's point guard?*" she asks incredulously.

I shrug my shoulders. "I guess?"

"I'm game, but Jesse is not going to like this. Although honestly, I think he could use a kick in the ass for ignoring you all night. Point me in the direction of that hot stuff."

I laugh as we follow the dirt trail down to the dock.

"Are you all ready to go?" I'm blinded by that smile once again.

"Yeah, I think so. Stephen, this is my friend Jade. Jade, this is Stephen." I point between the two.

"Hi, Jade, nice to meet you." He gives her the same swoon-worthy smile, and I'm pretty sure she's actually melting right here in front of everyone. I grab her arm and yank her towards the boat.

I hiss quietly at her, "Can you keep it together? I literally see some drool dribbling out of your mouth."

98

CALLIE RAE

"Did you see that smile?" Jade starts to fan herself with her hand. I roll my eyes and find a spot in the back corner of the boat.

Stephen finds us to offer us a drink.

"Do you have water?"

"Yeah, it's in the cooler towards the front. I'll go get it."

"As much as I want you and my brother to figure your shit out . . . girl, if you don't hit that, I will," Jade says, lifting her sunglasses up a little for a better view of him walking away. "Look at that ass."

"Jade!" I squeak. She chuckles. "You have my permission to . . . 'hit that,'" I say with air quotes. "I don't need to be involving myself with anyone any time soon."

"Good, because I have a feeling Jesse is going to be *pissed* when we get back. He was burning a hole in Stephen's head while you were talking to him earlier." She puts her sunglasses back in place as Stephen rejoins us with our drinks.

We hang out on the boat, chatting with Stephen and his friends. We all watch the sunset until it's dark, and then the boat turns back towards the shore and docks again.

"That sunset was beautiful," Stephen says as he helps me down from the boat.

"Yes, it really was. Thanks for letting us tag along," I say with a weak smile.

He tries to help Jade down but she stumbles out. At one point, she found a cooler full of these spritzers, I think she called them. About three spritzers in, she became a little sloppy.

"Whoops!" She cackles a little as she grabs onto me to steady herself.

"I better get her back to our cabin. Thanks again!" I wrap an arm around Jade, trying to support some of her weight.

"Hey, Fallon." I turn around to that damn smile again. "See you around?"

"Sure," I smile back.

CHAPTER SEVENTEEN

After a very bumpy and slow trek, we make it back to our cabin. I help Jade into her pajamas before getting her to bed. I put a trashcan next to her bed just in case she needs it, then I flop down on my bed and stare at the ceiling. Between the thoughts I have cruising through my mind and the empty space next to me, sleep isn't an option tonight. Lately, sleep has only been an option next to Jesse.

But I try. For an hour I lay there, counting the turns on the ceiling fan, listening to music, trying anything to shut my brain off. I give up when I reach fifty full turns and decide fresh air might help. I walk out on the porch, and inhale deeply. The air is clean here. You can't smell the hustle and bustle of modern life. The blue spruce trees nearby are so tall that I'm sure I could see a view of the world if I climbed to the top. The scenery is relaxing, and the break from life is soul-lifting. It doesn't turn off this brain of mine, just dampens it, but dampened is better than turned up, so I close my eyes and try to enjoy it.

"Can't sleep?" Jesse's voice interrupts my moment of peace, just like his swirly black eyes have interrupted my life. I open my eyes and turn towards his voice to find him leaning against the post on the porch watching me. He's shirtless and cut to perfection, which does nothing to help me get my head on straight. The black ink that swirls up his arm and onto his chest only makes it worse. The basketball shorts hanging low on his hips drive me wild with imagination. His presence drives me crazy.

"You know I can't," I say a little snappy. He stays silent for a moment, considering this.

"I saw you hanging out with that Stephen Rogers douche earlier." He narrows his eyes at me but doesn't comment on my attitude.

"Yeah, he took us to see the sunset on his cousin's boat."

Jesse smirks and shakes his head a bit, but then lifts his chin up. He seems irritated, but with what I don't know. He pushes off the post and stalks towards me, those black eyes never wavering. He stops in front of me, and the unease that I feel has me pushing my back into the railing. Jade warned me he wouldn't be happy about it. I should've listened. In a second, both hands wrap around my thighs and hoist me up. He deposits me on top of the railing and nestles his big body between my legs. His hands have me caged in, making it impossible to escape. This is exactly what he wants.

His jaw flexes as he considers his next words. "Seems like you used me and then rode off into the sunset with pretty boy."

"You wouldn't even look at me."

"So you jump in a boat with the first guy who comes along, to what? Get my attention?"

"I don't need your attention, Jesse." I narrow my eyes.

He smirks, his hands caressing my thighs. "Maybe not . . . but you want it."

"I want a lot of things. Most of them, I shouldn't."

He steps back and holds out his hand. I stare at it, confused.

"Come on. We both need sleep."

I shouldn't take his hand, or his offer. But as much as I shouldn't, I want to. So I grab his hand and follow him to his bed, where he pulls me back to meet his chest.

It's quickly becoming one of my favorite places.

When I wake, our arms and legs are still tangled together. Last night when we came inside, I realized the boys had separate rooms, whereas Jade and I only have one room. Jesse said it was because he didn't want to be in the same room as the Energizer Bunny, a.k.a. Cason, so he called ahead to make sure one of the cabins had two rooms.

The smell of coffee is wafting in and enticing me out of this warm bed. I want nothing more than to guzzle down a large cup of it.

I slowly pull away from Jesse. When I break free, he reaches for me before rolling over. His soft snores are still going strong.

The cabin is small, and as soon as I walk through Jesse's door, I'm greeted with a smiling Cason leaning against the counter with a mug in his hand.

"Any left in the pot?" I ask him.

"Yeah, there's a couple cups left." His voice gruff and hoarse. He must have partied too much last night. I reach for a mug off the counter.

"You ok? You don't look so good," I say while I pour my coffee.

He gives me a weak smile. "Yeah, I'm good. Just drank too much last night."

"I didn't hear you come in." I lean my hip against the counter and face him. I take a sip of my coffee, and warmth spreads through all of my limbs, making me happy.

So good.

"You wouldn't have. You were both sound asleep when I got here. Ya know . . . in the same bed." He looks at me, wiggling his eyebrows suggestively.

I sigh and put my cup down.

"We just slept. That's all. I sleep better when I'm . . . not alone."

"It's none of my business. I'll just say this—Jesse doesn't share his bed. With anyone. *Ever.* He has hooked up before, sure. But they never stay the night." He's waiting for my reaction to his confession. I swallow the hard lump in my throat. But my mind starts reeling. Does me staying the night mean something more?

It's just sleeping . . . right?

"Anyway, did you have fun this weekend?" His demeanor changes back to the easy-going, relaxed Cason I know and love.

"Yeah, it was nice being out here. I enjoyed the quiet. Well, when we weren't partying." I laugh. "What happened last night? You lost your game or something? I didn't think I would ever see the day when your bed was empty after a big party like that."

"Ha-ha, so funny. Just so you know, I may have found my way behind the boat shed with a pretty blonde cheerleader that just doesn't know when to stop."

I'm shocked. "You're not talking about—"

He cuts me off. "Yes, I am. There might be a video of her circulating when we get back. It could have already been released by now. Who knows?" The twinkle in his eye is alarming.

"You didn't . . ."

He gave me a gigantic smile that told me he probably wasn't lying. "I got you, Fallon." He winks at me.

"How did you get him up this early?" My head snapped up to the bedroom door where Jesse is leaning on the door frame, still shirtless.

For fuck's sake, put a shirt on.

"She didn't, but apparently the smell of fresh coffee grinds is all I need to get your girl out of bed." Cason laughs and I pretend I just didn't hear Cason call me Jesse's girl. That's not happening. Too soon.

Jesse walks over and reaches behind me for a mug. His hand grazes my back, and his chest rubs against my arm. He locks eyes with me.

"I woke up alone." His voice is so low I'm sure only I heard him.

I hold my coffee mug up and smirk. I see the corner of his mouth lift up. He reaches for the coffee pot and fills his cup. Taking a sip, he continues to stand so close that I can feel the heat radiating from his body.

"I guess I should go get Jade up if we're ever going to leave today," I mumble. I move to the sink to put some space between us. I place my mug on the counter and start mentally preparing myself for the fight I'm gonna face getting Jade up.

Jesse catches my arm before I can leave. "Are we good?"

I consider him for a moment and nod. "Yeah, we're good."

He releases my arm so I can leave, leaving a tingling sensation where his hand once was. But there's also dread building in my stomach, and I'm not sure what that means for me.

I walk across the yard, and when I reach my cabin door, Stephen is already there about to knock.

104

"Are you looking for someone?" I ask Stephen's back as he raises his hand to the door.

He spins around quickly to face me. "Oh, hey. I was trying to catch you before y'all left. I guess you caught me, though."

His nervous laugh was kind of cute, but he isn't Jesse.

He isn't Jesse.

I chuckle. "Yeah, I guess I did. So how can I help you?"

"Well, I wanted to stop by on the off chance that you would let me have your phone number."

"I don't know, Stephen, last night was fun and all but—"

"Just as friends. Promise," he says, pleading with his eyes.

I look back to the boy's cabin, considering this. He isn't Jesse, and that might actually be just what I need to get past whatever this thing is with Jesse.

"Ok, give me your phone." I hold my hand out. He quickly puts his phone in my hand, and I type in my number. He thanks me, promises not to text me too much, and hugs me goodbye. I face the door, and right before I go inside, I look back to the boy's cabin again. Jesse is glaring at me, both hands gripping the railing. He pushes off the rail and turns his back to me to go back inside, leaving me standing there.

Did I just make a huge mistake?

CHAPTER EIGHTEEN

The texts started on Monday. The first one was a simple "hi." Then came a rambling text on Tuesday about how it was from Stephen, and he should have said that first. That one made me laugh. Then the last one came through on Wednesday, asking if I wanted to get food with him. He assured me his intentions are purely platonic.

Jade and Cason have been picking me up all week without Jesse. Jade always has some excuse as to why Jesse wasn't with them, but I could tell she didn't believe them herself. I know why he isn't in the car every morning, and since he's already been ignoring me, I decided to take Stephen up on his offer.

Which is how I ended up here, on my bed, completely nauseous, and with Jade fanning me in my crisis. I'm not sure if this is even a good idea. I've considered canceling on him a handful of times, but Jade told me I need to go, that I need to know what it's like to go on a real date with someone sweet and kind. Personally, I think this is her way of sticking it to her brother for being an asshole all week.

Stephen will be here any minute. "This is a bad idea. What am I thinking? Just tell him I'm sick when he gets here."

She rolls her eyes at me. "This isn't a bad idea. This is a huge step for you. Have you ever gone on a date before?"

"No, unless you count a weekend party and my date puking all night as a date," I say, pulling myself together and off of my bed.

"Um. No. This will be a good start for you to figure out what you want for yourself." Jade wrinkles her nose a bit at the mention of puking.

"Kind of like you and Adam?" I ask. "When are you going to tell him that you like him?"

"That isn't the same thing." She looks down, picking at a non-existent spot on her pants. "Besides, he would have to notice me for me to tell him."

"Seems like he was noticing you just fine at the Bonfire."

The doorbell rings, and lucky for me, interrupts her next sarcastic comment. It doesn't matter, though, because I hit the panic button as soon as I hear the chime.

"Calm down. He even said it in the text—this is just platonic. Just go and have fun," she encourages me before leaving to go answer the door. I grab my bag and follow the voices coming from the kitchen.

I round the corner, and see Jade standing in the doorway, laughing at something Stephen has said. When he sees me, he stops mid-sentence.

"Wow, Fallon. You look amazing," he says as his eyes widen and drift down my bare legs. Jade put me in a drapey tank and black skirt, but I refused to wear the heels she brought. I put on my Converse, ignoring her protests. Jade's always protesting against my choice of shoes, so it no longer bothers me. Stephen seems to like it.

"Thanks. You don't look so bad yourself," I say. He really does look good. He has on a light blue button-up shirt and a nice pair of jeans. His look is casual but still kind of dressy, in a good way.

Jade basically has to push me out the door, but once I'm outside, I calm down enough to act like a normal human being.

Stephen takes me to a local Italian place. It's a cute little mom-and-pop restaurant. I order the baked ravioli and almost groan in pleasure when that first bite hits my tongue. We make small talk throughout the meal, and it's nice. He's a complete gentleman, insisting on paying the bill and walking me out. He even opens the car door for me and helps me into my seat, not that I really need it.

On the ride home, things turn a bit awkward when he reaches for my hand. I immediately jerk back when he touches me, not realizing at first that he'd just wanted to hold my hand. It's uncomfortable, and

I'm not sure how to explain myself without telling him my entire story, so we sit in awkward silence for the rest of the drive.

He pulls into my driveway and parks but doesn't move to get out. I stay seated, unsure of what to do with my hands.

"I had a good time with you tonight," he says.

Again with the awkwardness.

"Yeah, me too."

"Can we do it again sometime?"

In an effort to get out of this car before my nausea rolls right out of my mouth. I say, "Sure."

"Great. Here, let me get that for you." He jumps out and runs around to my door, opening it for me again.

He doesn't try to kiss me goodnight or any of that cheesy stuff. He gives me a stiff hug, and I all but run into the house, the urge to run away in full force yet again.

As soon as I get through the door, I have my phone out to call Jade and tell her just how bad it was. On the third ring, it picks up, but a deep familiar voice answers.

"Hello."

"Hey," I say, not sure what to say to Jesse.

"How was your date?"

So he does know.

"It was good." No way am I telling him it was horrible and awkward. "Where's Jade?"

Jade's voice comes through from the background as she yells at Jesse to give her phone back.

"Hello? Fallon? Hello?" she says, audibly out of breath.

"Hey, Jade" I say, but I no longer feel like telling her about my date. "I had a good time. I'm exhausted, though, so I think I'm going to get to bed."

"Oh, okay."

I can tell from the tone in her voice that she's disappointed. She wants the details as much as I'd wanted to tell her before Jesse answered the phone.

"See ya tomorrow," I say before hanging up the phone quickly. I lied—I'm not tired. I'm so worked up over the fact that Jesse knew I went on a date with Stephen, even if it was just as friends. Somehow, I don't think the friends part really matters to Jesse.

Did I just make another colossal mistake?

CHAPTER NINETEEN

It's now Friday, and my disappointment has turned into irritation. I don't care if he thinks he has reasons to ignore me—it's ridiculous. By the time Cason, Jade, and I arrive at a house party at one of the cheerleader's homes, I'm fuming over it. We walk through the wide-open front door, and I make a beeline to the keg. Drinking the week away sounds like a great idea. It only takes three beers before I'm teetering on the edge of my happy place, to the place where I can forget why I'm mad altogether. That is, until Jesse saunters in with a blonde bimbo wearing scraps for clothing, looking like Skanky Barbie. With the way she's dressed, she may as well be naked, because we could see almost everything.

Jesse doesn't look my way once. We're standing five feet from each other, and he doesn't even say hi. By the time I'm five beers in, my leg is shaking so fast that I'm ready to dump this entire cup over both of their heads.

"Jesseeee," Skanky Barbie whines, and her voice sounds like fingernails on a chalkboard. It makes me want to duct tape her mouth shut already. "Let's play beer pong! The table's open now," she whines again. My eyes roll on their own, but I'm pretty proud of it.

"What? Just me and you?" Jesse's voice sounds as irritated as I feel.

"You can play against Ruth and me," Cason speaks up, and then winks at me. "Come on, Ruth! We got this."

"I don't think—" I begin to say.

"Oh, yay! See, babe? We can play teams!" She rubs her hand across his chest, sweeping it under his jacket. I follow it with my eyes, wanting to vomit when she leans into Jesse, causing his shirt to lift up. I wrinkle my nose at the way she clings to him—like he belongs to her.

"If you don't fix your face, people are going to think you're constipated," Cason whispers in my ear, getting a small chuckle out of me. Only Cason would say something so dumb.

"So, what do you say, Fallon? Wanna play teams?" Jesse takes a sip of his beer, and his eyes lock on mine over the cup. He's challenging me. He's hoping I'll say no. It's written all over his face. I pull out the best "fuck you" smile I can find.

"Let's play."

We gather around the table. Cason is cleaning the balls and filling the cups up with beer and I anxiously wait for him to finish.

"Shoot for keeps." Cason tosses his ball and sinks it in the middle cup. Jesse drinks and shoots, and the ball bounces off the rim, rolling onto the table.

It's my turn, and I bounce it into a cup on the first try. "Yes!"

Skanky Barbie drinks it, unaware of her man's lingering gaze on me.

Cason and I are winning, while Jesse and Blondie are on their way to drunk-land. At this point, I have enough beer in me to throw away all my inhibitions. So, that must be why, when Skanky Barbie puts her hand under Jesse's shirt, I lose it.

"I mean, would you like me to clear off the table to make room for your little show?" I should just walk away . . . but, well, beer.

"Excuse me? What is your problem?" Skanky Barbie whines.

"Oh my God! You're my problem," I mimic her whining. "You might as well be having sex for everyone to see." I look up her up and down. "But from the look of you, I don't think you would mind that at all, would you?"

"Fallon. Enough," Jesse warns. I grit my teeth.

Walk away, Fallon, just walk away. It's not her, it's him, it's you.

That is what I should do, but instead, my eyes land on none other than Stephen Rogers walking into the backyard. I grab one of the cups of beer, down it right there, pick up another full cup and waltz my little butt right up to him. I'm being reckless but seeing Jesse with her makes me want to scream, and I don't understand it. I mean, it's not like Jesse and I are a thing. He can see whoever he wants.

But she isn't you. It should be you.

"Hey Stephen! I didn't know you were coming," I say, and wince a little when I touch his chest with my hand.

"Hey. I'm not going to lie, when my cousin called me about this party, I was hoping you'd be here." He places his hands on my waist, holding me upright, with his big, bright, beautiful smile on high.

"Well, here I am." I smile, throwing in a little wink.

"Yep, here you are. I'd ask if you wanted something to drink, but it looks like you have that taken care of."

"Yeah, I've probably reached my limit as it is."

"So, I don't want to scare you, but Jesse Callaway is glaring at us right this minute, and I'm not sure why."

I look back at Jesse, where he stands stiff as a board watching us. Blondie is still hanging off of him, and any fucks I would've given just flew out the window with her.

"Oh, he's mad I beat him at a game of beer pong. Don't mind him." I grab his hand, pulling him away from the angry god.

I stop in front of a swing set. Somehow I made it back here, but I'm not sure how. I think Stephen is holding me up. I decide the swing is an excellent place to sit down. The world is starting to spin, and I'm not sure standing is the best idea for me right now. Stephen sits in the swing next to me and we sit in comfortable silence for a while.

"So... you and Jesse, huh?" he says.

My head swings around to him, "What?"

"It's obvious from a mile away. His eyes were on you from the moment I walked through the back door. And then there are the glares I received at the lake." He chuckles.

"We aren't . . . together," I say.

"Yeah, look. It's none of my business. Just be careful with him. Trouble is always around him."

"What do you mean?"

"I . . . he . . ." He shakes his head. "Just promise you'll be careful."

"Yeah, sure. Ok." I nod. "I think we should probably get back to the party."

"Here, let me help you." He stands up and holds his hand out.

"You know, you really are a great guy. " I peer up at him.

"But? There's always a but," he says with a half-smile.

"But nothing. You're a great guy," I say.

"Just maybe not the guy for you?" Stephen says.

I sigh. "I just need to figure some things out. Friends?"

"Sure. Friends." He smiles but it doesn't quite reach his eyes.

We begin the trek back to the party, but as soon as we come around a shed into view, Jesse grabs Stephen by the collar and slams him into the wall.

"Jesse!" I scream. "Stop it!"

"Do not fucking touch her again. You hear me?" Jesse's growl is menacing.

"Hey, man—chill out. We were just talking." Stephen reaches up and pulls Jesse's hand from his shirt. "You two need to talk. I'm not the one you're angry at."

Stephen looks to me. "It was good seeing you again. Good fucking luck with this one." He motions his head towards Jesse, who's still standing in his face, fuming. Stephen walks away, leaving Jesse and I facing each other in a tornado of confusion.

"What the fuck was that?" I yell.

"What the fuck was that? What the fuck is *this*? What were y'all doing behind the shed?" he yells back.

"None of your damn business, Jesse. What have you and Skanky Barbie been doing while I was gone?" I throw back at him. *Two can play that game.*

"Skanky Barbie?" Jesse shakes his head. "You went on a date, Fallon. With someone other than me! What was I supposed to do, wait for you to wake the fuck up and see what is right in front of you? I can only pretend we don't have something happening between us for so long."

"You don't want me, Jesse. I'm not like these other girls in high school. I've got issues, a lot of them. You don't—"

114

Jesse quickly pulls me to him, crushing his lips to mine. I freeze, unable to comprehend what's happening right now. His tongue grazes my bottom lip before he gently tugs it down with his teeth to allow him access. He's kissing me so hard that if I let go, I'm likely to fall. It's perfect. Our lips line up just right, our tongues dance in perfect harmony, and my toes curl when he deepens it. I'm mush in his arms, and all it took is one perfect kiss.

He pulls his head back but still cages my face with his hands. I'm out of breath, and my lips are tingling. He looks straight into my eyes, unblinking, and says, "That is how our first kiss should've been."

Then he walks away. And I let him go as I touch my tingling lips. *Did that just happen?*

CHAPTER TWENTY

I follow in Jesse's footsteps, in desperate need of Jade. Instead of just Jade, I find Jade, Jesse and Cason huddled together. I get close enough to hear Cason's worried and hardened voice.

"Jesse, we have a problem." Cason is bleak and masked off entirely from the outside world. It's so strange to see on such a lively person. Jesse tenses up the moment Cason speaks. "I just got a text from Shady." Cason's eyes become hard and angry.

"It's her?" Jesse asks.

"What's going on?" I ask.

"Stay out of it, Fallon," Jesse snaps at me. I close my mouth, fuming on the inside—but something tells me this is not the time to be rebellious. Something serious is going down.

"Jesse." Cason places his hand on Jesse's shoulder. "It's time, man. We have to trust her."

For a moment, they meet each other's eyes. Silent words pass between them without even one syllable pronounced. Jesse nods, but with reluctance. He's wary about whatever Cason wants to share with me. Cason drops his hand from Jesse's shoulder as they all turn to look at me, Jade included.

"You've never asked me why I live with my aunt and uncle. How come?" Cason asks. The vulnerability he's allowing to filter through makes me nervous.

"It isn't my business. I figured if you wanted me to know, then you would tell me." I shrug my shoulders as if this entire moment isn't so intense that it has me shaking in my spot.

Cason gives me a sad smile before taking a step closer to me. "The thing is . . . my birth mother is an addict. She has been in and out of jail for as long as I can remember. James and Catherine took me in when I was fourteen because her neighbors didn't see her for a week, but they saw me coming and going and knew something was off. They became worried. They came to check on us, and they found my mother lying on the floor in a pool of her own vomit while I was at school." Cason swallows hard, pausing to gather himself. I look into his eyes and see moisture pooling. I can't just watch him struggle, so I grab his hand in encouragement. He looks at our joined hands, giving mine a quick squeeze. I'm aware of Jesse's eyes on me, the tell-tale tingle on my neck letting me know he sees my gesture of support. "CPS doesn't care for addict parents and put me in my aunt and uncle's care. I've been there ever since. The last time I saw her I got a call from an unknown number. It was some dude telling me to come get my mom because he didn't want her to die on his couch. When I got there, the guy had a needle in her arm while she was passed out. I had to bring her to the emergency room. She was released within a few days, only to go right back out on the streets."

"What about your father?" I ask Cason.

He lets out a sardonic laugh. "I don't know who he is. I'm not even sure she knows."

"Has she gone to rehab?"

"She's been in several. She never stays. As soon as she can, she voluntary discharges herself." Jesse volunteers the information when he sees the struggle in Cason's eyes.

"She just goes for as long as she needs so the court will drop her charges," Cason adds.

I'm not sure what, if there even is anything, I could say to make this better. Instead, I simply show support by wrapping my arms around Cason and holding him tightly.

"I'm so sorry you've had to live like this," I whisper to him. He slowly wraps his arms around me. Jesse and Jade remain still as they watch this moment unfold. Cason's tender soul needs this right now.

"I'm so afraid that I will find her one day, dead from an overdose." His distraught voice waves over me as he clenches his eyes shut. "And that'll be it. No more mother. It's so stupid, because she has never been much of a mother anyway."

I pull back from him, taking his face in my hands. "It's not stupid, Cason. She's your mother, and she has a problem—a disease—but that doesn't mean you're not allowed to still love her. You just have to love her a little bit differently than you love the rest of us."

His nostrils flare as he nods his head slowly. I pull away from him, facing all of them. "So, what do we need to do tonight?" I ask. It's my own way of letting them know I'm not going anywhere.

"She's at The Depot," Cason tells us.

"Why is she there? It's mostly kids." I wrinkle my nose.

"Jax." Jesse meets me with a murderous glare.

"Why would she be with Jax?" Jax is a dealer. She's an addict. I widen my eyes and look to Jesse. "That's why you walked away?"

Jesse gives a curt nod as Cason sighs. I look at each of them. They're family, and they're letting me in on a big part of their life. But what is even more shocking to me is that I think I'm accepting their offer.

"Ok, so what do we need to do?" I ask

"Just like that, you're down?" The amazement in Jesse's voice coming across clear.

"Just like that, for Cason." I hold my voice and my eyes steady, daring him to question me. We face each other down. Jesse needs to know I'm serious, so I hold my gaze strongly to show my unwavering loyalty to Cason. To this family.

"Let's go then." Jesse nods in the direction of the house. As we begin to walk towards the car, Jesse purposefully hangs back a bit to walk next to me.

"Thanks." Jesse speaks quietly as we watch Jade and Cason walk ahead of us. Cason's head is hanging low.

"For what?" I ask.

"For what you just did for Cason. He doesn't like to talk about it with us. I think he feels like he's betraying us by wanting to be there for her."

"I wonder why he would get that impression from you, Mr. I-Walk-Around-Hating-The-World." I bump my shoulder into him as I joke. He chuckles a bit, but it sounds as sad as his chosen brother's laugh. His eyes stay on his brother's back; he's worried about Cason. It's obvious in his furrowed brows and the visible sadness in his stance when he thinks no one is watching.

"He deserves more," he mumbles, more to himself.

"You all do," I say.

We reach the car. Jade is already sitting in the back seat. Cason is holding the seat forward, waiting for me to climb in. I meet Jesse's eyes over the roof of his car; despite the intensity of our earlier moment, I knew we are on the same page. We are going to leave it all behind us to fight tonight, for Cason.

CHAPTER TWENTY-ONE

The ride to the Depot is quiet. All of us are anticipating a fight. Jesse called a few more of his boys to meet us. They beat us there and when we arrive, the crowd parts to let Jesse park upfront. It still amazes me how much authority he holds over people. Of course, the stares begin as soon as we step out of the car. Jesse leaves the vehicle first, leading the way towards a crowd lingering on the side of the long, dirt-filled track.

"Jesse Callaway. What did I do to warrant a visit from the prince himself? Here to race?" A woman—with an average build, short brown hair, and makeup covering every inch of her face—asks. Her false nails are at least an inch long, and her clothes look no bigger than the size of a hand cloth. I definitely don't have to wonder if her boobs are fake.

She walks right up to Jesse and slides a hand up his neck to the back of his head. Her plastic boobs are almost in his face. Jesse pulls away casually to put space between them.

That's right, he isn't interested.

She glances at me before shaking her head and chuckling. She didn't miss it either.

"Shady, this is Fallon." He throws his thumb over his shoulder to me. She nods her head to Jade and Cason, and when she gets to me, a smirk covers her face like she knows something I don't.

"I'm not here to race tonight. You know why I'm here." Jesse looks at Shady pointedly.

"Yeah, I was afraid of that. They got here about an hour ago and have been sitting at the end of the track watching the races." She nods towards the finish line.

"Did they say anything to you?" Jesse steps into her space and lowers his voice.

"You know I can't tell you that. It's bad for business and Daddy Callaway doesn't like it when the money isn't flowing. If I start snitching on the guys, they'll stop coming out here. What I can tell you is that he hasn't moved from that spot since he got here. But plenty of people have gone down that way to hang, if you catch my drift." She's trying her best to give him what he needs without saying it.

He nods, "Thanks, Shady."

"You got it. Alright, I have a job to do. Y'all don't have too much fun without me." She winks at Jesse.

This is much worse than Skanky Barbie back at the party. I think I'm beginning to hate my own kind.

Jesse guides me with his hand on my back as we make our way towards the end of the track. Unfortunately, we don't have to go far for Jax to make himself known with a handful of his guys. He was clearly expecting us. Jesse pulls me behind him. Cason does the same with Jade. I try to look over Jesse's shoulder, but he reaches behind him to grip my waist, holding me in place and making it so my only view is of Jax's head.

"Callaway. Funny thing seeing you here." Jax smiles almost sinister like.

"Where is she? And why the fuck are you on my property again?" Jesse gets straight to the point.

"Don't worry, little Callaway, Momma Cruise is right over there chilling out. And last time I checked, you don't own this property. Or has that changed?" He points behind him to the bed of a truck where someone—I think it's Cason's mother—is slumped over in a heap. Cason's pupils dilate and his hands ball up into fists, but he doesn't go to her like I know he wants to.

"You damn well know this is mine. What do you want? You're not selling out here to these kids."

Jax laughs at this. "That's what you think this is? I don't think you quite get what's happening right now. But my boy here would be more than glad to straighten things out." A hooded figure comes forward slowly through the crowd until he stops next to Jax. I can't see under the hood, and Jesse tucks me a little closer into his back, making it impossible.

"You remember him, don't you, Cason?"

Jesse hisses under his breath just as Cason jumps forward, but the guys Jesse called for backup are on Cason in a beat, holding him back. Jordan tries to talk Cason down, and I don't like it, but it'll have to do for now.

Another voice speaks up, and I freeze. I could never forget that voice. It's the voice of my nightmares—the shadow that lurks looking to destroy me. "Your mom here, well, she has been quite the entertainment tonight."

No, no, no, no, no...

I start shaking my head into Jesse's back, gripping his shirt. Jesse tenses, glancing over his shoulder.

"You son of a bitch, I'll kill you. I will fucking murder you right here!" Cason is screaming, giving Jordan and the guys holding him back a rough time.

"Now, now, that wouldn't be very nice." My blood runs cold.

"Fuck you," Jesse growls.

Cason breaks free and reaches for the guy. Jesse leaps forward, grabbing Cason and leaving me standing there exposed to the man I never thought I would see again. My hands tremble as I lift my eyes to him. I can see my worst nightmare from here. It's him. It's Marcus.

"Fallon? Are you okay?"

My eyes fill with tears. *No, No, No, No, No.* I start shaking my head. This time Jesse looks to me and worry lines his face.

"Fallon? What's wrong?"

I just keep shaking my head. My body is slowly pushing me back, telling me to run fast and hard, to not look back.

"Oh, Fallon, baby, what an unexpected surprise." Marcus actually smiles. I take another step back.

"Fallon?" Jesse calls again. The confusion on his face is evident.

"Oh, this is good. You and him?" He points from me to Jesse and laughs. "Well, you never were good at picking them. So, tell me. How's your mother? I'd heard you moved here, but I never expected it to actually be true." He's goading me, I know it—but then, he always was so good at manipulating.

I stare at him, taking another step back.

"Ah, I see, you're not quite over our last . . . run-in."

My eyes snap to his. He doesn't get to do this anymore. He doesn't get to control me. He doesn't get to talk about that day like it was nothing. I can feel my breathing hammering my lungs, and I clench my hands in an attempt to steady them.

"Don't you dare talk about it like that, like it's nothing but another day. It wasn't just another day." I can feel the fire returning to my veins. I take a few steps forward to where a confused Jesse is now standing next to a dumbfounded Cason.

"You're a sorry excuse for a human being," I spit at him.

Jax takes this moment to laugh. "Man, this is some good shit. Y'all know each other? I brought him out here to shake you all up, but this is even better. Your bitch has baggage, Callaway. Who would have guessed? Maybe Marcus could show her how it feels to be knocked around, since she seems to like to play with pipes and all."

Jesse freezes.

He knows who I am.

"Wait, this is who hit you with the pipe?" Marcus looks surprised.

"Yeah, little bitch sneaked me. Bad move, little girl," Jax taunts.

"You leave her out of this. I had the pipe," Jesse gets out through his clenched jaw.

Jax steps up in his face. "Or what? You'll have your little bitch fight for you? Next time you come at me, you better come at me hard. You feel me?"

A gunshot pops off, and we all drop to the ground. People are scattering to their cars leaving just Marcus and Jax facing us. I turn towards the sound to see Shady standing there with a rifle.

"Now y'all know fights are bad for business, so I just can't let you do that. You both got about nine minutes, if I had to guess, to get you and your guys off the property before the law shows up. I'd advise ya to get yer asses in your cars and get the hell out of here." She looks so

124

comfortable facing down a pack of men. I have to give it to her—it's badass.

We get to our feet now that we know there isn't a real threat. Jesse has me by the arm in an instant, damn near dragging me.

"This isn't over, you piece of shit," Cason yells at them as he runs to his mother, lifting her out of the bed of the truck and over his shoulder. She moans a bit when he throws her over his shoulder, but she is otherwise incoherent. An almost evil cackle hits me in the chest; it's the same one I hear in my dreams nearly every night.

I shake my head to clear it just as we reach Jesse's car. He all but throws me in the passenger seat of his vehicle after Jade and Cason dive into the back seat, Cason's mom in a slump on his lap. Jesse slams the door shut and rounds the hood, getting behind the wheel in a flash. He hits the gas, spinning his tires as he reverses. He slams the car into drive and tailspins the hell out of there. His grip is so tight, his knuckles are white. It was less than five minutes after we left that we start to hear the sirens in the distance.

She really did call the police.

He's pushing the speedometer when a flash of blue and white passes; the car then makes a U-turn in the road, coming after us.

"Jesse, he's turning around," I yell.

"I know. Stay calm, it's alright."

"How is this alright? You're going like, twenty over the speed limit. Why are we even running from the Depot? Your father owns it."

"Fallon," Cason pleads. "My mom has warrants out. Please just stay calm for us."

I turn right in my seat and tap my hands on the armrest as Jesse pulls over. "Just let me do the talking. Nobody say anything."

The officer is quickly approaching the car, but Jesse pushes the car door open with his hands where they can see them. The officer stills and asks Jesse to come to the back of the vehicle. I can't see much through the tinted windows, but this can't be good.

"He knows what he's doing, Fallon," Jade's soft voice breaks the silence.

"Just trust us," Cason affirms.

I watch them, fearless all because of their brother. Another police unit drives up now, and the panic really sets in.

"He was going way too fast. They are going to take him to jail," I whisper.

"He's fine," Jesse interrupts as he gets back in the car.

I watch as both of the units begin to drive off towards the Depot. "What? How?"

Jesse puts the car in gear, pulling onto the road again and ignoring my question.

"Your boy here holds all the power. The police department's biggest donor happens to be the Depot. Which is exactly how we keep them off our backs out there," Cason mumbles from the back seat.

I sit forward in my seat, breathing deeply and trying to calm my body. The reality of everything that has happened settles over the car, leaving everyone in painful silence. This nightmare keeps replaying in my head. Finally, Jesse slows down when we're far enough away from everything that's haunting me. He drives back to the party and drops Cason and his mom off at his Jeep. Jade goes to get out too, but stops to turn back to Jesse.

"I'll see you at home?" Jade asks.

Jesse doesn't look at her, but he gives her a nod. I barely get back in the car and shut my door before Jesse is taking off again.

CHAPTER TWENTY-TWO

He hasn't spoken to me since we left the Depot unless necessary. Even after dropping Cason and Jade off, he has remained quiet. He's bringing me to his home, but he's driving slower than usual—stalling. He jolts me out of the silence when he punches the steering wheel a few times.

"What the hell was that Fallon?" he yells out.

"I . . ." I shake my head, trying to organize my thoughts so I can make a complete sentence, but my mind seems to have shut down on me. It can't handle anymore.

"How do you know that guy?" He doesn't look at me. I don't think he can right now.

"His name is Marcus." I sigh. "Do you remember what you asked me in the car the day you took us to the rope swings?"

"What are you talking about?" The frustration radiates off of him in waves.

"Think about it. What did you ask me?"

I see the wheels turning as he thinks back to that day until his eyes widen, and I know he remembers.

"I asked you who broke you. It's him? Marcus?"

"Yes, Jesse. He's the one who broke me."

We pull into his driveway behind Cason's Jeep, and he throws the car in park. Neither of us makes a move to exit the vehicle.

"How bad is it?" He whispers.

I sigh. "Come on, let's go inside. I can only tell this story once."

We walk into the house, and my eyes find Cason first. He's standing in the middle of the living room, pacing. I felt the sob bubbling up before the tears began. Something about seeing Cason so anxious and worried pushes me over the edge.

"Cason, I didn't know he was involved. I'm so sorry." With tears streaming down my face, I shake my head.

Jesse grabs hold of my hand in an effort to comfort me. Cason stares back at me, unwavering in his stance. Pain flashes through his face, and before I know it, he's holding onto me like his life depends on it.

"Shhh, it's not your fault. I believe you," he coos in my ear, like he's comforting a small child. It only makes me fall apart more. There is no way this sweet boy is comforting me when it's I who should be comforting him. I back away and wipe my tear-stained face with my sleeves. I try to regain as much composure as I can to do what I have to do next.

I pull both of the boys to the couch. They sit one on each side, Jesse's grip holding strong in my hand. Cason's hand finds my knee as I face Jade, who sits on the coffee table in front of me. I prepare myself to tell a horrible story.

"How is she?" Jesse asks Cason about his mom and I know it's to give me a moment. Jesse doesn't care about that woman. But I appreciate him trying to give me what I need.

"She's good. She's sleeping it off in my room."

Jesse nods before all eyes turn on me. I take in a big gulp of air. I'm about to relive everything I've been pushing down for the last year.

"I guess it's time for me to share a story of my own." I take in a deep breath and run a shaky hand through my hair.

"Fallon. It's alright. Take your time. We aren't going anywhere." Jade reaches across to hold my free hand. I look at these three people who forced their way into my life and became my only lifeline in this

128

journey. I'm about to do something I never would've thought I would be capable of ever doing again—I'm going to trust them with my soul.

"About a year and a half ago, my mom and I lived in a small town about two hours from here. I had a perfect life—good grades, played softball, and was on the homecoming court. I smiled all the time and I had so many friends. I guess you could say I was popular." I give a weak laugh because I don't even know who that person is anymore.

"All was going well. I met a college boy, and we started dating. He was so perfect, always doing and saying the right things. I was swooning over the fact that I was a junior in high school, and he was in college. We were always together after school and on the weekends. I . . ." I squeeze my eyes shut, taking a few deep breaths, pushing the sobs down so I could get through this.

"He was my first real relationship. First kiss, first . . . everything." I swallowed and looked up to Jesse. He didn't react, but I can see the pulse in his neck. I'd prefer he keep his mask in place because anything else will keep me from finishing. "I was a stupid girl. I let him talk me into not using a condom. The next month my period didn't come. I went to my mom and told her that I thought I might be pregnant. She took me to the doctor the next day. They confirmed it. I was a month along."

Jesse's grip on my hand tightened, but that was the only tell that my words affected him.

"I told him, but he didn't want anything to do with it. He called me a whore and said I'd cheated on him when I had only been with him, and he knew it."

"I . . . I was alone. All I had was my mom. She was wonderful. She never judged me. I think she judged herself as a parent more than she did me. She went to every appointment with me. When I told her I wanted to keep the baby, she didn't even blink—she just started making plans to make the guest room into a nursery." I couldn't hold the sobs in any longer, I cradle myself in my arms and rock.

I can't do this, I can't finish.

"What happened, Fallon? You don't have a baby. We've been to your house. It's just you and your mom," Jade speaks, her voice low and steady. She was trying to hold it together for me.

"Marcus happened, didn't he?" Jesse is the one to speak now. I turn my face towards him and look him in the eyes. A murderous glare stares back at me. He's the one I worry the most about.

"What did he do to you, Fallon?" Jesse lifts me onto his lap and wraps me up. I grab onto his shirt and hang on for dear life.

"He . . . He . . ." I take another breath trying to steady myself, but another sob escapes anyway. I squeeze my eyes shut and just breathe. They all wait for me to gather myself. This part is the hardest for me. This part almost killed me. It definitely killed what was left of my heart.

"He took her from me. He followed me one night, and he beat me until I couldn't feel anything and just left us there to die. I was six months pregnant, and he just took her. Said that he couldn't have me walking around with his kid. That I should've terminated the pregnancy when I'd had the chance . . ." Jesse's fists clench around me, his hold only getting tighter.

"Someone found me and called an ambulance, but by the time I got to the hospital, it was too late. I had lost so much blood. She was gone. I delivered her that night . . . stillborn." I close my eyes and focus on breathing, my breaking heart shredding me to pieces.

"I held her in my arms and named her Luna. A few days later, I buried my sweet baby girl. After that, I couldn't handle it anymore. The stares and whispers, or the thought that he could come for me at any time. So, we moved. Apparently, not far enough away. How fucking ironic is that?"

"I'm going to fucking kill him," Jesse growls, his grip so tight on me I can't move. His body is trembling underneath me, and I know it's taking everything he has to remain seated right here with me. Because he knows that's what I need from him at this moment.

"Oh, Fallon . . ." I look to Jade, she has big, fat tears falling for me. The tortured expression laid across her face is too much, and I have to look away.

"Fallon, I swear to you he will pay for all the sadistic shit he has done to you. Marcus will not ever touch you again." Cason's eyes burn with a fire I'm not sure anyone could ever extinguish. He's going to end this one way or another—there is no doubt about it. It's how he will end it that scares me, and who will help him. I don't want either of them getting into more shit because of me.

I answer all of their questions until we are all just too tired and emotionally spent to keep going. I find out that Marcus is the guy that Cason walked in on putting a needle in his mom's arm. I shudder when Cason explains this to me. Marcus has hand-fed the toxic drugs running through Cason's birth-mother's veins. He has had a part in taking away the only parent that boy had left. This helps me reach for my anger, replacing my misery with something I can focus on: making sure that Marcus can never touch us again.

Jade convinces me to stay there since it was already early in the morning by the time everyone is ready to go to bed, so I use the guest room across from Cason's room. She makes sure to point out her and Jesse's rooms to me. I make sure to text my mom that I'm fine and at Jade's. I tell them all goodnight and close the door behind me.

I lay there for at least an hour staring at the ceiling. I'm exhausted after our long night, but I can't close my eyes. I'm afraid of reliving my nightmare, and I really just can't go through it again. Not alone.

I get up and tiptoe out of my room. I shouldn't bother him. I should just go to Jade's room and leave well enough alone. But my feet take me straight to his door, and before I know what I'm doing, I knock. I hear feet shuffling, and then the door creaks open slowly. He leans on the doorframe in nothing but shorts. His shirtless body is on display for me, and I can't help but notice all of the muscles and ridges that fold throughout his abdomen. When I greet his stare, I bare all of my emotions on my face. He refuses to look straight at me; his eyes are on the wall behind me for a beat or two. But then he heaves a tired sigh and takes my hand to lead me to his bed.

We fall into our usual position: my back touching his chest, his legs tangled with mine, and his arms wrapped tight around me. I'm talked out, but he has one more question for me.

"The moon tattoo on your arm. That's for Luna, isn't it?" Jesse's breath drifts across my neck in a shiver.

"Yes. I got it a week after I buried her. I couldn't feel anything, and I thought maybe I would feel that. It just made the ache worse at first."

"How?"

131

"It was a permanent reminder of what I was missing. Now I take comfort in it. Almost like wherever she is, she's calming me."

He pushes my hair back from my shoulder, and I relax even more into his arms. The lull of his steady breathing allows me to finally find sleep, but it's his arms wrapped around my body that push my shadows away.

CHAPTER TWENTY-THREE

Life continues on after my big reveal. We all fall back into our regular routine with Jesse back in the driver's seat every morning. In the afternoons, Jade and I make it a habit to stay and watch their practices so we can all ride home together, except on the days that she has cheer practice. Some days I go to their house, and some days I go to mine. We haven't spoken about Marcus or my past since that night. I really think it's because playoffs are coming up, and the team has doubled up on practices. I don't mind. My mom seems really happy that I'm out with friends more. They all decided to come in one afternoon to hang, and my mom gushed over them. When she thought Jesse was out of earshot, she let me know how dark and handsome she thinks he is. I saw a hint of a smirk when I turned to him that told me she wasn't as quiet as she might have hoped. I'm pretty sure my cheeks had never been that shade of red before.

One afternoon, Jade left with some of her cheer squad friends to, "go shopping," as she put it, so that left me to ride home with Jesse alone. Cason brought his Jeep because he had a date with a girl after school whose parents were out of town, leaving her house empty. That's just code for he's going to hook up with her.

Jesse is hungry after a hard practice and wants to stop for Chinese on the way home. I'm not going to argue; my stomach is growling louder than a rumbling train. My apple at lunch really didn't hold me over. He brings us to this quaint little restaurant that has a typical Chinese buffet and the instrumental versions of today's popular songs playing overhead. The music here has always made me laugh; I mean, imagine the Backstreet Boys songs with only instruments, no voices. Anyone would laugh at the ridiculousness of it.

The weirdest thing happens when we walk through the doors: the hostess immediately starts calling out to Jesse.

"Jesse! Jesse!" she says, her excitement evident. She's an older Chinese woman, and her English is broken, but she's a beautiful lady.

"You want usual?" she asks.

Does he come here often enough that they know him this well?

"Yes, Mrs. Chen. Thanks." He gives her his best smile.

"Oh, you bring date. Come, we give you best spot." She waves us on with our menus and silverware in her hand. A blush is spreading through my cheeks at her mention of date, because this is so not a date. She sits us in a booth in the back with low lighting surrounding us. It's cozy, which I think is her intention for our . . . date.

I pile food on my plate until it starts to fall off the sides. We both end up going back for more several times, making us look like starving kids.

"Were you hungry?" he asks, laughing at the three empty plates before me.

"A girl's gotta eat!" I laugh with him.

"I know, but most girls eat like a rabbit in front of guys."

"Most girls aren't me."

Jesse lifts his cup to salute me before placing the straw in his mouth. "Touché."

The corner of my mouth lifts slightly, but I can't hold my smile in for very long before I'm full-on grinning stupidly at him.

"Now, you just need to drive a truck to make sure you really stand out from all the other girls."

"Nah, I don't even know how to drive. I think a truck might be too much for me."

Jesse's eyes bug out of his head as his jaw drops to the floor.

"What do you mean you don't know how to drive? Do you not want to get your license?"

134

"I guess I never really had a chance to get it given everything that happened. And sure, I want it. But I just don't want to bother my mom. She works a lot to take care of us and has done a lot for me in the last year. Including dropping everything to come here." I drop my eyes to my lap. I'm still not used to speaking so openly about my past.

Jesse pulls his wallet out and throws some cash on the table. He picks up his drink, taking one more sip before standing up, offering his hand to me.

"Come on. Let's go." His hard eyes stare down at me.

I sit frozen to my spot. "Where are we going?"

His face slowly transforms as it lights up. A glint in his eye that tells me he is up to something.

"We're going to teach you how to drive."

And he was serious. He brought me to an empty parking lot, put me in the driver's seat of his car, and told me to press the gas. Then yelled at me to stop.

"Ok, let's try this again. Slowly press the gas." Jesse grabs his oh-shit handle on the roof of his car.

That doesn't make me nervous at all. Ok, I can do this. Just press the gas slowly.

The car lurches forward a bit but then smooths out as I make circles around the parking lot. I laugh. I'm actually driving!

"See, you're doing it. Okay, let's practice parking. Pull into that spot right there."

I turn the car into the direction he points, taking it extra slow to make sure I pull in between the lines.

"That's it. You did it!" His excitement is infectious, but the way his face is lighting up for me . . . it's better than driving. He's beautiful. Is that thing? Finding a boy beautiful? Because that is the only way I can describe him in this moment.

I match his contagious grin with my own as I place the car in park. A giggle bursts out of me, and I have no idea where it comes from. I slap my hand to my mouth, embarrassed that I just giggled like a girl. I mean, I *am* a girl—just not one that giggles over a guy.

"Okay, now drive us home." Jesse pulls his seat belt on adjusting in his seat.

I stare at him as if he's crazy. No, I take that back—there is no if. He's legitimately crazy.

"I can't drive us home! I don't have a license!" My voice comes out in a squeak.

"And you won't ever get one if you can't be comfortable on the road. So, drive us home." He motions to the gearstick, then crosses his arms. I stare at him. I'm not ready to drive on the road.

He grabs the lever on the side of his seat and leans it all the way back, wiggling a bit. "I guess we can get comfortable, because we aren't going anywhere unless you drive us there."

He closes his eyes as I continue to stare. I look at the clock on the dash and curse. It's getting late; we both need to get home soon.

I send a silent prayer up to the sky and pull the gearstick into drive. My grip on the wheel is so tight that my hands are aching. I press the gas and steer the car to an opening to the road. I stop right before the street and look both ways. Jesse is still pretending to take a nap in the passenger seat.

No cars are passing by, so I go for it and pull out into the road, staying to the far right. Then I breathe out and channel my inner Jade by releasing another squeal.

I'm doing it! I'm driving on the road! Entirely too slowly, but I'm driving!

Eventually, Jesse sits up. He doesn't say much except to tell me to put my blinker on or where to turn. I bring us all the way to my house safely. By the time we arrive at home, I'm more comfortable behind the wheel. I don't know how he knew I needed to do this, but I'm sure glad he did.

I toss the car into park and look to Jesse. "We made it."

He smirks, giving me a quick nod before opening his door to get out. I get out as well and meet him in the front.

I stand awkwardly as he looks to me. "Um, thanks for that."

"Sure, no problem. Next time will be even better."

"I don't know about that. I should probably wait until I get my license." I snort.

"At least you're considering it now." He shrugs.

"Yeah, I guess I am. All right, I should get inside. Thanks again." I wave before stepping backwards toward the direction of my house.

Jesse smiles as he leans against the front of his car, watching me back away. I wave goodbye before turning around to waltz into my house on a high. I can feel his eyes on me until I step through the door. I glance back as he finally gets into his car. Shutting the door, I touch my forehead to the cold surface. My heart is smiling.

What am I doing?

CHAPTER TWENTY-FOUR

As I walk down the hallways at school, I notice all of the prom posters and banners on the walls. I never understood the hype around it. Every girl is freaking out at the possibility of being asked to go to the dance with one of the guys. Jesse and Cason are a hot topic right now as the cheerleading squad and the entire female student body wonder who the captain of the basketball team and his sidekick are going to ask. Elizabeth has been falling all over Jesse. He is enjoying it about as much as he would enjoy a foul egg being broken over his head. I lean against Jade's locker just in time for her next attempt at getting her paws on Jesse.

"I can't watch it. Her pathetic attempt at getting my brother makes me want to vomit." Jade rolls her eyes as she puts her books in her locker. I laugh just as Jesse pulls Elizabeth's hands off his chest shaking his head to her. I'm not sure what he says, but it has her storming past us.

"Why don't you find someone else to whore around with? I hear you're easy to get behind a shed anyway," Jade calls after her. She turns to Jade and scoffs. Now I'm really laughing. Jade flips her off as we meet up with Jesse, and annoyance flashes on his face as he watches the exchange between the two.

"I'm not going to make it to prom. Today I had cupcakes waiting at my locker and a red card shoved in the crack with so much perfume on that it's permanently burned into my nose." He wrinkles his nose.

"I just don't get it." I shake my head.

"It's just a reason to get all dressed up, drink, and have sex," Jade says roughly.

"Oh, whatever. You're just mad Adam Clarke hasn't asked you to the dance yet," Jesse chuckles.

Glaring at him, Jade sneers, "Like you know anything." She storms off.

I sigh as I watch her go. "You shouldn't tease her like that."

"What did I say?" he asks, an expression of mock-innocence on his face.

I can't help but smile at him. "You know exactly what you did. She's already upset, and now rumors are going around that Adam is going to ask one of the girls on the dance team. If your sister doesn't have a date, she is going to be devastated. You know that, right?"

"Oh man," he groans. "It is really tough being her twin sometimes."

"Ha, imagine how she feels." I laugh at him as I turn to walk away.

"Hey, now. You didn't mind me the other night in my bed," he says way too loudly. I turn back and slap a hand over his mouth.

"What are you doing?" I hiss.

"Solving all of my problems." He winks at me as he starts to back away from my hand, leaving me standing in the middle of the hallway in complete disbelief. This is his way of getting me back for the beach, and he just gave them all something more to talk about.

He knew exactly what he was doing. This is probably why I have to borrow a used gym uniform since mine magically up and walked away when I got to the locker room to change. By the end of the day, most of the cheerleading squad is glaring daggers at me, and some even pass by coughing out a "slut" or a "whore." It's all very original.

I wait at the car after the last bell with my sunglasses over my eyes, still feeling aggravated with Jesse.

"Ruth! I heard a rumor about you and Jess-man today. Wanna know what that was?" Cason walks up and puts his arm around me.

I groan. "I'm going to kill him."

140

"Could be worse. You could have gotten caught banging in the coach's office by the janitor." His smile beaming at me. Then he winks.

"I don't even want to know," I say as Jade and Jesse walk up.

"You don't want to know what?" Jade asks

"Nothing. Absolutely nothing," I say, getting in the back seat.

CHAPTER TWENTY-FIVE

Cason turns the radio up, blasting a rock song I'm not familiar with while singing his little heart out. I'm in the back with Jade, who is submerged in her phone, texting. I glance in the mirror, meeting Jesse's gaze. I've caught him glancing at me a few times now. Every time he does, my stomach betrays me with a little flip.

The ride home is unusually quiet except for Cason's music. As we get closer to my house, I notice a cloud of black smoke rolling in the sky. It's pretty in a gloomy way. I hope nothing important is on fire.

"Fallon!" Jade's frantic voice broke through my daze.

"What's wrong?" I look at her, then follow her gaze.

"That's your house." Her wide eyes point ahead to bright lights flashing and the fire trucks lined up the street. The feeling in my gut isn't right as Jesse pulls to a stop behind a police car.

I don't even let Cason get out—I climb over him and jump out of the car, disregarding Jades pleas behind me. I run towards my house hard and fast. I get to the carport before I'm lifted off the ground.

"Mom!" I scream. Tears stream down my face as I try to thrash out of the strong hands holding onto me.

God, please be okay.

"Where is my mom?" I scream out to anyone who will listen.

"Fallon. Look at me, Fallon." I hear the voice, but I'm too focused on getting to the door. Jesse's face comes into view, and I breathe hard. Something in the air isn't right.

"Where is she!"

"Fallon, you can't go in there!"

"Let me go. I have to find her!" I kick and push.

Why he won't let me go find her? Doesn't he understand?

"Dammit, Fallon." He growls, and the next thing I know, his lips are on mine, and he's kissing me hard but steady. He isn't gentle as he forces my mouth open with his tongue. My heart rate slows, bringing my panic down a notch.

Wait, my mom! I pull away from him.

"My mom . . ." I swallow hard, still trying to catch my breath in this thick fog.

"Will you listen to me now?"

My nostrils flare as I regain control of my breathing. He has about three seconds, or I'm running in.

"Your house is on fire. You can't go in there. But I overheard one of their radios say they found your mom and are bringing her out. I don't know what kind of condition she is in, but Fallon, I need you to calm down."

Smoke . . . I smell smoke all around me.

I start for the door again, but his firm grip holds me in place.

"Fallon, you *cannot* go in there. It's not safe."

He's lucky that a fireman appears in the doorway carrying my mom in his arms. She's covered in black soot. It's on her hair, her face, her clothes. The paramedics act as soon as she's clear of the house, immediately placing an oxygen mask on her. Jesse lets me go this time as I run to the stretcher they set her on. Relief pours over me when I find her still conscious.

"Mom? Are you okay? Mom?" I can barely see through the tears running down my face. I can feel the warm wetness on my shirt. My entire body is trembling from fear. The only thing I can think about is losing my Mom too. I hate the way it makes me feel helpless and hopeless.

My mom rolls her head back and forth. She's mumbling something, but I can't understand her.

"Mom, I'm here," I say as I place my ear closer to her to listen.

"Marcus . . ." I think I hear her say. The blood drains from my head as my stomach drops, and I think I sway a bit.

"What about Marcus Mom?" I say slowly, squeezing her hand tighter. The paramedics are pushing her into the ambulance, and I climb in, thoroughly planning on staying right by her side.

"Marcus . . ." she says again. But she begins coughing, her chest wheezing with every gasp of air she grabs.

The paramedic pushes me out of the way to listen to her chest with his stethoscope. I sit in the corner and watch him work on my mom, my vision becoming dreamlike. Voices are muffled, and I feel like at any moment, I'll wake up. This must be what shock feels like. I'm responsible for this, for my mom laying on this stretcher. *This is my fault.*

When we arrive at the hospital, the nurses and doctors take her behind closed doors and escort me to a chair in the hallway. One of the nurses stops by at some point and hands me a warm cup of coffee. I jump every time the door opens, and watch medical staff going in and out of her room for what feels like hours. I ask each person I can for an update, but so far, they've only told me that she's stable.

A police officer and a fireman come by to tell me that the bedrooms were completely gone but that my mom saved the rest of the house by shutting the doors before she tried to get out. The officer, Officer Greene, claims the fire is suspicious and they are investigating it as a potential arson, making my home a crime scene. He tells me no one is allowed to enter the area and that it was taped off. He proceeds to ask me too many questions that I have no answers to. Jesse walks in during the middle of the questioning, and it doesn't take long for him to get irritated enough to tell the officers to leave. I don't hear what else he says, but they leave soon after.

"Fallon, hey. Are you okay?" Jesse's voice gently prods me out of my fog. He softly grabs my chin, turning me to him.

When I see his eyes, something in me breaks. The tears flood my face.

"This is all my fault, Jesse." He pulls me into his chest, letting my tears fall on him.

"This is not your fault," he whispers.

"But it is. She told me . . . She said . . ." I choke on the words.

"Shhh. We don't have to do this right now."

"Excuse me. Are you Darla Blake's family?" A woman in scrubs appears. I wipe my eyes and lookup. I recognized her as one of the nurses who met us at the ambulance.

"Y—yes, I'm her daughter," I stammer out, giving up on composing myself.

"Your mom is awake and asking for you. You can go see her for a few minutes, but she really needs her rest." She walks back to the door but stops when she realizes I'm not behind her. She waves her hand to encourage me to follow. I stand, but Jesse quickly grabs my hand, standing up as well. I don't take the time to think about it. I just squeeze his hand harder, letting the nurse lead us to my mom. His grip is the only thing comforting me in this chaos. When we get to the door, the nurse stops Jesse, explaining that only one visitor is allowed at a time. She said that my mom is weak and can't handle more than that.

I let go of Jesse's hand, and hesitantly enter the hospital room. My eyes fall to my mom lying in the hospital bed. Her leg is in a sling raised up slightly, and an oxygen mask covers her face. They've taken off her soot-covered clothes and put her in a hospital gown. It looks like they've also tried to clean up her face a bit, but she still has black streaks in her gray hair. Just seeing her weak body lying there pulls at my heart. She lifts her hand slightly off the bed, reaching out for me. I quickly move to her, grabbing her hand with as little pressure as possible while still holding on for dear life.

"Hi Mom. How are you? Are you okay? Oh, Mom, I'm so sorry!" The tears start again as soon as I open my mouth.

She reaches up and pulls the mask down so she can talk to me.

"Baby, don't you do that . . . don't you . . . blame . . . yourself," she says between coughing fits. I bring the mask up to her face, allowing her to take a few deep breaths.

"Shh, Mom, just breathe." I run my hands through her hair.

She pulls the mask down again once she catches her breath, determined to get her point across, even if it's a lost cause.

"It's not . . . your . . . fault." She takes a few more deep breathes in her mask. "You did not . . . do this."

146

"But Marcus—he wouldn't have done this to you if it wasn't for me."

"Marcus is . . . sick . . . and twisted. That is . . . not . . . your . . . fault." She stares at me, narrowing her eyes, trying her best to make sure I understand her intent.

A knock comes at the door, and the nurse peeks her head in. "Sorry, but your mom really needs her rest. You can come back in the morning at eight when visiting hours start."

I nod to the nurse then turn back to my mom. My sweet mom. I kiss her on the cheek, repeating three little words. "I love you."

Before I leave, I promise to be back first thing in the morning. Jesse is right where I left him, waiting for me. The nurse tells Jesse to take me home and explains the visiting hours to him. He looks to me to make sure that is what I want before he guides me out to his car. He puts me in the seat and straps me in like I'm a kid again, which is fitting since my brain is functioning on the same level as a toddler. I don't have anywhere to go, so Jesse brings me back to his house. As soon as we step through his front door, Jade and Cason attack me with hugs and whispers of their support in my ear. The tears start all over again, and this time I cower from my friends. It's too much for one night. I think Jesse realizes this because he tells them he's taking me to bed and says we can talk more tomorrow.

He doesn't even bother bringing me to the spare room; we go straight to his room.

"Fallon, you have soot all over you. You really need a shower." He walks me into his bathroom and turns the shower on, waiting until steam starts to rise out of it.

"I'm going to see if Jade has any clothes you can borrow." He walks out of the bathroom, and I hear the bedroom door click. I walk over to the shower and remove my soot-covered clothes. I pull back the curtain, and slowly step inside the steamy shower. My body feels heavy with the weight of the night's events, my legs like lead. The water hits me, and my body sinks to the floor. I use the shower wall to hold myself upright as I drop my head to my knees. I don't think I can handle much more.

I'm not sure how long I stay like this, but eventually I realize the water has gone cold. I hardly notice it; there's a numbing that seems to accompany cold showers and lost thoughts.

I ignore the rapping of knuckles on the door.

"Fallon, are you okay?" Jesse's voice drifts in over the water.

But I can't answer him, so I just stay where I am, numbing the pain.

The door clicks open, and Jesse calls out to me again. "Fallon?"

I don't know how long it takes for him to make his way into the bathroom. It's all starting to run together: the fire, my mom, Marcus, Jesse. I need it to stop; it all needs to stop.

"Fallon!" I hear him shout when he finds me.

"Shit, the water is cold." He reaches up and shuts the water off. He quickly grabs a towel off the rack and wraps it around me.

"You're freezing." He begins to rub the towel down my body. I think I hear a chattering noise, but I can't figure out where it's coming from.

"Oh, baby." He bends down, jostling me a bit until I'm floating in the air. He quickly deposits me under the covers of his bed and proceeds to start stripping his wet clothes off down to his boxers.

"W—what a—aa—re y—you d—doing?" I ask through chattering teeth, realizing just how cold I really am.

He doesn't answer me, but instead slides in and wraps his arms around my naked body.

"We need to warm you up. Your lips are blue." He rubs slow circles on my back. The heat radiating from his skin slowly begins to warm me, and with that warmth comes a flood of thoughts.

"I . . . it was Marcus."

Jesse stills. "What was Marcus?"

"M—Marcus started th—the fire."

Jesse sucks in a breath that sounds eerily similar to a hiss. "Get some sleep, Fallon. We will figure this out in the morning."

"Okay." The shivering has finally ended, and a yawn escapes my mouth. I'm suddenly exhausted and don't find it too difficult to drift off to sleep, even after the events of the day.

"Shhh. She's still asleep. Don't wake her up." I hear a growling whisper from Jesse.

"She's going to want to go to the hospital to see her mom," Jade whispers.

I stay still and keep my breathing even. I'm not ready to face them yet.

"I know, but she needs to rest. She doesn't sleep well on a good day, and you didn't see the way she looked when I found her on that bathroom floor," Jesse snaps in a hushed tone.

"Jess." Jade's voice comes out soft now.

"She's blaming herself, Jade. She thinks Marcus caused the fire and that it makes her responsible for what happened to her mom."

I can't listen to this anymore.

"She is awake and can hear you," I say in frustration.

"Oh, sorry, Fallon." Jade uses that same comforting tone on me as she comes to sit on the bed next to me. "How are you feeling?"

"I need some clothes, and a ride to the hospital." I look past her to Jesse. He nods.

"Jade, can you go see if you have something she can wear?" Jesse asks.

"Yes, of course. Do you need anything else?" She turns to me.

"Maybe a toothbrush?"

"You got it. I'll be right back." Jade saunters out, leaving her brother and me staring at one another.

"So, I'm sorry about last night. I . . ." I feel my cheeks heat up. Jesse's eyes roam down to the sheet covering my body, and I feel a little more self-conscious than I did last night. I pull the sheet tighter around me, avoiding his gaze.

"It's fine. You just had me a little worried."

"Th—Thanks for taking care of me. You didn't have to."

"I wanted to." My head snaps up to look at him. I'm sure my entire face is tomato red by now. "Fallon, I—" Jesse takes a step towards me, his eyes burning into my skin.

Jade walks back in with an arm full of clothes and a toiletries bag that looks far too laden down to hold just a toothbrush.

"I brought you some choices, and I figured you might need a hairbrush and a few other things," she says, utterly unaware of the tension in the room.

"I'll let you get ready. Meet me downstairs when you are ready to go." Jesse backs out of the room, and I watch him go. I don't want him to leave, but I'm not brave enough to admit it.

"Do you need any help?" Jade interrupts my thoughts. I look at her and shake my head.

Jesse.

"Ok, well, I'll be downstairs if you need me." She goes to leave but pauses at the door.

Jesse.

"Fallon?" She turns back around, worry lining her eyes. "Don't hurt him. He wears the weight of the world on his shoulders. And I think you have the power to bring it all tumbling down."

Do I have that kind of power over him?

Jesse.

I nod, not sure what else to say to her. She's worried about her brother, and she should be. She would go to war for him, but I would go to war for all of them. These people have become like family to me, and that terrifies me. But what scares me even more is what I would do for *him*. Because here I am, filling my head full of thoughts about him, when I should be focused on getting to my mother who's lying in that hospital bed for no other reason than because she has me for a daughter.

Jesse.

150

CHAPTER TWENTY-SIX

My mom has been in the hospital for a week now. I've been staying at Jade and Jesse's house in their spare room. I've considered Jade's warning and put some distance between Jesse and me. The police haven't made much progress. I tried to inform them about Marcus, but they didn't seem interested in pursuing him since my mom couldn't remember much about that night. They haven't officially ruled the fire as arson yet.

Cason brings me back to their house after a long day at the hospital. We walk through the front door and are immediately met with the aroma of something cooking—and it smells amazing. I look to Cason in question, and he has a sloppy grin on his face. We don't make it far into the house before a woman dressed to the nines encases me in a hug.

"You must be Fallon. I've heard so much about you." She's beautiful; her children's dark locks cover her head, but Jade's soft features stare back at me.

"Oh, uh . . . yes ma'am." I stand still, stiff as a board in a very awkward, not-sure-what-to-do-with-myself sort of way. Jade had always said that their parents travel for business all the time, and I hadn't expected to meet either of them. Ever.

"Oh, I'm so sorry! You probably have no idea who I am. I'm Catherine. Mom to those three mischievous kids running around here somewhere." She pulls away from me enough to allow me to breathe but keeps her hands on my upper arms.

"Hey Momma C. Is that corn chowder I smell?" He reaches for her and pulls her into a tight hug. I'm not sure Cason realizes it, but he's never lacked a mother, just blood.

"It sure is. Go ahead to the kitchen. It's almost ready." She gives him the most loving smile a mother could give her child.

"Come on, you two. I'm sure you are starving for some real food. I know these three survive off of pizza and takeout when we're away." She gives my arm an encouraging squeeze, and somehow my body works enough to trail Cason into the kitchen. Cason wastes no time in filling a bowl and slurping it down at the kitchen table.

"Mom, is that you?" I hear the front door close and look back to see Jesse walking towards us.

He goes straight to his mother, wrapping his arms around her and lifting her off the ground. Just being in her presence make his face lift into a smile that brightens the room. It's beautiful to watch them love so freely.

"Alright, that's enough. Put me down, son." Catherine laughs, and he does as she asks.

"Is Dad here?"

"He is at the office right now, but he'll be home later."

"Oh, Mom, did you meet Fallon yet?" he asks, turning back to me.

"I did. I may have swarmed her as soon as she came through the door." She smiles at me.

"Are you hungry? I cooked corn chowder."

"Ooh, yum. I am, but I need to go shower first. I just got back from the gym."

"Okay then, you go get cleaned up. We'll be down here. Fallon and I can get to know each other." I didn't like the hint of mischief in her eyes, or the smirk on her face.

"Go easy on her, Ma," he scolds. I stare at their mom, possibly seeing two heads. "She's had a rough week. Please." He gives his mom a look that I'm not sure I understood. He almost appeared to be pleading with her.

"Don't you worry about us. We'll be fine." She winks at me. "Isn't that right, Fallon?"

Jesse comes over to me. Leaning in so that his breath tickles my cheek, he whispers, "Are you good?"

I meet his eyes, and the concern there catches my breath. I nod, still trying to find my head.

"I'll be okay." He runs his eyes over my face searching for any doubt. He nods when he seems to find whatever confirmation he needs from me. He kisses the side of my head then leaves us sitting together alone, while he goes off to enjoy a nice shower. Once he is out of sight, his mother chuckles and looks me over.

"I told you," Cason says.

"So you did. Fallon, would you like a bowl of soup?" Catherine pulls a bowl out and starts filling it before I answer. She sets it down on the table and pulls out a chair for me. She waits for me patiently, but I suspect I don't actually have an alternative option here.

"It's not poisoned, if that is what you're worried about." She smiles again. Well, I can see where Cason gets his sense of humor from. I sit down, accepting the fact that I'm going to have to deal, whether I like it or not. She looks determined to talk to me.

She sits next to Cason and looks at me, tilting her head in assessment.

"Fallon, why don't you tell me about yourself?"

"I'm out." Cason picks up his bowl, walking out.

Catherine yells what I'm thinking: "Chicken."

We stare at each other for the next few minutes. She appears inviting, and it eases me into almost wanting to share with her. Almost.

"What would you like to know?" I mumble in between a spoonful of soup.

This stuff tastes amazing.

"Well for one, why does my son feel the need to protect you from his own mother?"

I spit a mouthful of food out.

"You thought I didn't notice?"

I give her a weak smile. "I keep wondering why as well. Although he doesn't give me much choice."

She laughs at this. "No, I suspect not. He's a stubborn one, but he sees something in you worth protecting, and that tells me more than anything you could say at this table."

"Then why give the impression you wanted to talk?"

"To see my son squirm. It's payback for all the hell he put his father and me through as a child." She smiles, and, given the way her face lights up the room, it's obvious that Jesse gets this ability from his mother.

"My children told me about your house and your mother. I just want you to know that you and your mother are welcome in our house for as long as you need it. It's not like we don't have plenty of room." She snorts, and this makes me love her even more.

"Thank you. I really appreciate that." My eyes mist up as I think about being homeless.

"Oh, honey!" She pulls me in for a hug, one of those mom hugs that you can sink into, one I didn't know I needed until now. Even if it was from a complete stranger.

When Catherine releases me, I give her a nod to let her know I'm okay.

"I'm going to take a shower. Thank you again," I say, quickly standing and placing my dirty soup bowl into the sink before spinning on my heel and hightailing it towards the stairs. The tears are threatening to spill over.

I take my time in the shower, trying to gather all my loose strings back together. My emotions are hanging all over the place. When the water starts to run cold, I finally give up and get out.

I quickly dry myself off with a towel before wrapping it around my damp skin. When I re-enter my room, Jesse is sitting on the edge of my bed, wearing nothing but a pair of gym shorts. His head hangs low as he leans forward, his elbows balancing on his knees. His mouth is tight, his eyes are narrow, and his posture is tense. He's here to confront me. I lean on the door frame and take a few seconds to let my eyes roam over his body. The muscles in his back are more prominent in this position. His arms are manly and look strong. His hair is tousled from running his hands through it. I sigh, and his head snaps up to meet my gaze.

"What are you doing?" He lifts his eyebrows.

I go to the dresser to grab a shirt and a pair of shorts that I bought earlier this week to have something to sleep in.

"What are *you* doing?" I throw his question back at him.

His eyes follow me around the room. "I just wanted to check on you. You've been distant all week."

I pull the shirt over my head and shimmy the towel down.

"I don't know what you mean."

I pull a pair of boy-short underwear out of a drawer and put them on.

Jesse stands up and makes quick strides across the room. He cages me in with my back to the dresser.

"Don't pull that crap with me, Fallon. You're avoiding me. Why?" He clenches his teeth as his arms tense around me.

I stare down at the floor, avoiding meeting his stare.

"I don't know what you want me to tell you," I almost whisper.

Why is this so hard?

He cups my chin and brings my gaze back to his.

"I want you to tell me the truth," he growls.

I close my eyes and take a deep breath in through my nose.

Why does he have to smell so good?

I take a few moments to gather my strength before opening my eyes to face the only guy that can affect me in this manner.

"I can't do this." I push through him and grab my shorts, heading to the bathroom. Looking for an escape.

He grabs my arm before I can get too far and turns me back to him. "The fuck you can't do?"

His mouth clenches, and if I look hard enough, I can almost see the red covering his pupils.

"This. Us. I can't do this. This can't happen." I think I yell this, but my chest is so heavy I can't focus on anything else. His shock doesn't bring me out of it, and I think it only makes it worse.

"So, what? You're out before it even starts?" He throws his hands out to his sides, palms up. He's expecting me to answer, but I don't have one for him.

"Can you just go?" I croak out. I look away. A twenty-pound weight just found its way on top of my already-heavy chest, topping it off like the cherry on a sundae, suffocating me.

He nods, walking to the door. But he doesn't cross the threshold. Instead, he leans both hands on either side of the door frame. I see the muscles flex in his back as he considers something. He turns his head to me and pushes away from the door.

"Whatever is going through that mind of yours, there is one thing you're failing to realize." His eyes narrow. Flames lick around in there.

"What's that?" I grind out.

Pinning me with his hard stare, he plainly states, "You became mine the first moment you walked into my school." He turns abruptly and leaves me with a slam of my door. I jump a little, bringing my hand to my chest. I fall onto my bed and place a pillow over my face, and I scream into it as loud as I can.

Why can't anything in my life be easy?

CHAPTER TWENTY-SEVEN

I've been spending all of my time at the hospital with my mom, who's now fully awake and sitting up. She has burns on one third of her body, a broken leg they suspect is from falling while she was trying to escape, and she inhaled quite a bit of smoke so her lungs will need time to heal. They put her in a regular room so I can visit and stay overnight. I've been sleeping on a cot the last two nights, which helps me avoid facing Jesse again. In an even larger attempt to avoid him, I've asked Jade to stop by to bring me clean clothes.

"Do you want me to put a pillow behind your back, Mom?" I've been sitting next to her bed while we watch soap operas. There isn't much for her to do while just lying there.

"Sure, baby, that would be great." She smiles at me with her generous blue eyes. I fluff the pillow up and help her slowly lift. She winces a little, but she tries to hide it so I won't worry. Some of the burns on her back and stomach make it hard for her to bend.

"There you go." I smile weakly.

She pats my hand. "Thanks, baby. But you don't have to take care of me all of the time. You know I have nurses that are being paid to do just that. The night nurse even sneaks me extra Jell-O." She winks. "If you want to get out of here and go hang out with your friends for a little while, that would be ok."

She's always worrying about me, even after knowing I'm the reason she is here in the first place.

"No, that's ok. I'm good right here with you." I turn back to the TV.

"Fallon." The no-nonsense tone of her voice means serious talk. I try to prepare myself. "I hope you know that none of this is your fault."

I gasp. "How can you even say that Mom?"

I stand up to put a little distance between us. "Look at you. This happened to you because of my choices. Marcus did this to you, to our home, to hurt *me*. You wouldn't be here if it wasn't for me." My voice cracks, matching my insides. They are cracked wide open and seeping out.

"That is simply not true. You cannot control that boy any more than you can control the weather. I'm here because he is an evil person. The only thing you can control is what you do going forward. I will not have you sitting here sulking because you think this was your fault."

"I—" I start to argue, but Jade just happens to walk through the door at the same time.

"Hey. So, your clothes are in the bag. And I thought maybe you would like to go try dresses on with me today. Just for a little while." She places the bag on the floor and looks up at us. She tenses when she feels the tension in the air.

"Oh, sorry. Am I interrupting something?" she asks, looking back and forth between my mother and me.

"Of course not. This is as good a time as any. Come, give me a hug." My mom motions to her, and she does just that. Jade's body relaxes; a hug from my mom can do that. She just has something about her that makes everything okay. Jade sits on the edge of the cot in front of my chair. I plop back down into the chair, getting myself prepared for them to gang up on me about leaving.

"So, what is this about a dress? Do you have a date?" my mom asks cheerily.

"Fallon didn't tell you? Prom is tomorrow. I thought maybe we could go get Fallon a dress."

"No, no way. Not with my mom lying in a hospital bed. Besides, I don't even have a date."

"Oh, honey, you have to go! It's Prom, and it's your senior year. I will be fine. I have soap operas and these trashy magazines to keep me entertained."

158

"Besides, you can go with me. I don't have a date either. Come on, Fallon. Please? I don't want to go alone." She juts out her bottom lip and clasps her hands together in a pleading gesture.

"We can't even afford a dress right now. It's not a good time. Just drop it." I shut it down, closing myself off from them emotionally. My mom looks disappointed, and Jade's expression matches. It's enough to almost make me change my mind.

"Okay, well I better get going. You can call me if you need anything, alright?" She goes to hug my mom one more time and waves to me as she walks out. Guilt swallows me whole. I know I'm not being a good friend to her, but my mom is all I have—I need to be here for her.

We wake up to another full day of soap operas. Mom was a little uncomfortable throughout the night, but she did well to try and hide it. The doctor came by to tell us if Mom's burns keep healing as well as they have been, she may get to go home in two weeks. Being as we don't have a home anymore, I don't really know where we will be going, but I'll figure it out. For her.

"Honey, do you think you can run down to the cafeteria and get me one of those fruit cups?" my mom asks.

"I mean, they have room service here Mom."

"I know, but that usually takes them a while, and I really would like one now." My mom smiles.

"Yeah, I guess so. Do you have the remote to call the nurse if you need it?"

My mom pats the blanket on her side. "It's right here."

"Okay, I'll be right back."

"Thanks, honey!"

Reluctantly, I leave her alone and go to the elevator.

A fruit cup? I guess this is good, right? She's getting her appetite back?

There is quite a line already when I get to the cafeteria. I get through the line as quickly as I can, every part of me screaming to get back to my mom. I try to hurry back, but the elevator happens to be on the very top floor. I bounce my foot, willing the elevator to go a little bit faster.

I finally get back to my mom's room. The door is slightly cracked, and I know I shut it behind me. The nurse must've come by. I walk through hesitantly, rounding the corner to find her sitting up in her bed with a flat white box in her lap.

"Mom?" I ask.

What is that in her hand?

"Here. It's for you." She pushes the box towards me.

"What is it?" I ask, moving towards the bed.

"I'm not sure. It just arrived while you were out."

I set the fruit cup down on the side table and sit on the edge of her bed.

"There's a card." She hands it to me. I open it with shaky hands.

Put this on and be ready by seven. P.S. I'm solving all of our problems.

I hand the card over to my mom and reach for the box. I untie the big bow and lift the lid slowly. I see a spot of dark green peeking out from under the tissue wrapping. I gasp when I pull back the rest of the tissue paper. He bought me a dress. Jesse bought me a dress, and it's perfect. I pull out the most beautiful dark green dress I've ever seen. It's a princess dress with a V-neck top that plunges. It's sexy, but not so much that it's too revealing. On each side are two thick straps on an A-line cut. I'd never be able to afford something like this.

My phone beeps, distracting me from my surprise. I pull it out of my pocket and read the message waiting for me.

Jade: The purple case at the bottom of the bag. You're welcome. ☺

Me: Thank you, but I can't take this. It's too much.

Jade: Try telling that to Jesse. I don't think you are getting out of this one Fals.

Jade: See you at 7! 😊

"So?" My mom asks. I look up to her, in shock.

"It was Jesse."

"Jesse?" My mom looks as confused as I feel.

After standing there, completely transfixed, for a few seconds, my mother says impatiently, "Well, what are you waiting for? Put it on. Let's see what it looks like." She claps her hands together in so much excitement it would be impossible to deny her. I go to the bathroom to slip the dress on, and as it slides over me and into place, I realize that it fits me perfectly, almost as if it was made just for me. I come out of the bathroom, twisting to fix the back.

"I'm not sure if I can get the hooks in the—" I look up and stop in my tracks when I see my mom in tears. "Mom, are you okay?"

The urge to go to her almost turns into panic.

"Oh, honey, I'm fine. That dress looks gorgeous on you."

I look down at the dress and then back to her. "Mom, I can't accept this dress. It's way too expensive."

She narrows her eyes and tightens her lips. I know this look. I sigh. She's going to fight me on this.

"You will accept this dress, and you will go. Do you understand me? Now let's talk about Jesse. What is going on there?"

I groan. "Nothing mom. Absolutely nothing." I sit in the chair and lean back.

"Doesn't look like nothing to me. This dress is gorgeous. Boys do not think about buying girls these kinds of things—not unless there is something there."

I'm not sure what to say. I don't really know what is going on there. But this dress? It means everything.

Guess I'm going to prom.

"Will you do my make-up?" I look back to my mom, and her eyes light up. Her smile grows so big I think her face is going to crack.

"Of course, I will. But your hair . . . We may need some help."

Mom does my make-up, and she calls in a nurse to help with my hair. I tell her not to, but she insists that she is a patient and needs help. It doesn't take much convincing once the nurse sees me in the dress. She also raves about how my mom is the best patient she could have. When all is said and done, I have a high ponytail that drapes curls down to my shoulders.

I look in the mirror and hardly recognize myself. My mom highlighted my eyes with a pretty green shadow that I'm sure Jade snuck in my bag, and she lined my eyes with a charcoal grey. The nurse gave me winged eyeliner, saying all the girls are doing now. It's now close to seven and time for me to go downstairs. I text Jade to let her know I'll be waiting.

"Take plenty of pictures!" my mom says as I hug her goodbye. I give the nurse a hug as well, for being so great to my mom and me.

"Thank you for helping us."

"Of course. Anything for this amazing woman." She motions to my mom, making me smile behind misty eyes.

Less than five minutes after I get downstairs and to the front of the hospital, a white limo pulls up to the curb. The back door opens, and Jesse gets out in a black tuxedo. Against all of my willpower, my eyes roam over him. His hair is swept back with hair gel, and the tux fits his shoulders perfectly. When my eyes lift back to his face, I realize he's doing the same to me.

He takes a few steps toward me. "Fallon . . ." He swallows visibly. "You look . . ."

"He means you look amazing in that dress." Jade's head pops out of the limo. "Can we save the lovey-dovey stuff for later? I don't want to be late."

Jesse rolls his eyes at his sister while holding his hand out for me. He pulls me close for a brief moment. I've missed his warmth. He lets me slide into the limo first, and I find Cason with his date, who I'm pretty sure is a Junior. Jade is with Adam, which is a shock to me. She was dateless as of yesterday, according to her.

Jesse's body heat envelopes me when he slides in next to me. I turn to him, and lean in. "Thank you for the dress. You didn't have to do that," I whisper so only Jesse could hear.

162

"She told you." Jesse looks over at his sister, who is enthralled by whatever Adam is saying to her.

"She didn't have to. You are the only one who would have done this for me. Besides, who else would use me to solve all their problems?" I meet his gaze. A shiver runs down my back, through my legs and stops at my toes. He reaches for my hand and pulls it down on the seat between us so the others can't see. With my palm up, he slowly runs his fingers up and down the length of my hand, and then repeats the movement. By the time we pull up to the school, all my nerve endings are tingling, making me all too aware of how much I've missed his touch.

I'm so screwed.

CHAPTER TWENTY-EIGHT

Prom has an Italian theme this year. We enter the gym, and it's like walking the streets of Italy. There are backdrops on the walls of old Roman monuments that I remember from one of my history classes. The photo area has a backdrop of a gondola appearing to float on a canal that passes under a Venetian bridge. There are lights on the ceiling that sparkle like stars. White trees with twinkling lights wrapped around them surround the faux-cobblestone-covered dance floor. Small round tables line the walls on either side of the gym. Each one is decorated with a flower arrangement and candles. The room feels like a romantic scene from a movie.

"Adam, why don't you and the guys go get us drinks? We'll go find a table," Jade suggests with big puppy dog eyes that have him wrapped around her finger, making him agree in less time than it took for her to ask.

Cason grumbles and gets a nudge from Jesse, and all the guys walk across the gym to the back table where the punch and finger foods are.

Jade pulls us over to the nearest empty table while Cason's date leaves us to find to her friend's table. I sit with a sigh, giving my feet a break from the heels I'm not used to wearing.

"I can't believe you came. I'm so happy for you. And did you see my brother? That tux looks great on him." Jades face is bright and happy. She's grinning from ear to ear with excitement. And she's right—Jesse does look good in that tux. It fits him in all the right places. My gaze finds him, and I slide my eyes over the strong outline of his back as he stands next to the table talking to the guys. He glances over his shoulder at me as though he could feel my stare. He's smiling until he sees my face. When our eyes meet, a fire burns in them. I swallow, looking away. I can't handle that kind of need right now. Not when my feelings are so jumbled up inside my head.

I turn back to Jade with the best smile I can muster up. "You got me here, and I'll be damned if I just sit here."

I eye the throng of people dancing with a grin. I hope this will give me a little bit of relief from all the tension built up inside.

"Oh, hell yes! Let's go!" Jade squeals and yanks me onto the dance floor. I begin to dance as I let the music flow through me. I'm trying to find any distraction from all of life's crap.

We dance until our feet hurt and we're breathing so hard I'm certain Jade might turn blue. We hold each other up as we stumble back to our table. Jade trips in her heels and almost takes me down with her. We giggle as we continue navigating our way through the seating area, and eventually make it back to our table.

The guys are all sitting around. Jesse is on the far left, resting his elbows on his legs and watching me. I try to ignore his stares, but when Jade takes a seat next to Adam, leaving only one chair left—right next to him, of course—I'm left with no other choice but to face him. As soon as I'm sitting, he leans towards me, letting his cologne fill my nostrils and making it entirely too hard to ignore him.

"You seem lighter tonight." His voice flows like silk, sliding over me. I don't agree or disagree, I just don't respond. A slow song comes on over the speakers, and Jesse looks up like he can see the music floating in the air. He stands, holding his hand out to me.

"Dance with me?" I look at his throat, not wanting to look him in the eyes, afraid to see what he might be showing me in them. His Adam's apple bobs up and down as he swallows. We're on display for the entire table, and they are anxiously awaiting my answer. I nod and brace myself for a peek at his face as I place my hand in his. His back is to the dance floor, and he walks backward, pulling me to him. His gaze never leaves my face, even when we make it to the middle of the dance floor.

He tugs me into his embrace, and my body molds into his, causing friction I rarely let myself feel with him. By the way his nostrils flare and his breathing becomes uneven, I can tell he feels it too. His free hand finds my back as I slide a nervous hand slowly up his chest and onto his shoulder. His corded muscles tense at my touch. He begins to guide us into a sway, always leading, and the steady beat of my pulse finds its way to my fingertips. With every sway of his body I become more aware of him. The wakes of those touches leave tingles all over. Just one look from him fills me with need. Even if my brain wanted me to walk away from him, I know my heart wouldn't allow my feet to follow. But my mind isn't telling me to walk away like it should. My doubts all fell away the moment we touched and now, with the way he looks at me like I'm the only girl in the room, it all feels like too much.

"What are you doing, Jesse?" I whisper.

He leans into my ear, and his warm breath tickles my neck. It takes everything I have from giving in to the shiver that tries to envelope me. "I'm dancing with you."

I close my eyes. "You know that's not what I meant."

He sighs and stops moving. With quick hands, he grabs my chin and tilts my head up to face him, just as I squeeze my eyes shut. "Open your eyes, Fallon." I brace myself for the storm brewing in him and slowly open them, meeting his gaze. "You asked me what I was doing. I knew what you were asking. And the truth is, we have been dancing around each other for a while. You can try to avoid it all you want. You can try to pretend like your breath doesn't catch when you see me, that your entire body doesn't tingle from my presence."

He slides his hands up, over my shoulders, and onto my neck until his hands are cradling each side of my face, and I close my eyes again, reveling in the way his hands feel on me. "You can pretend that you can't feel your racing heartbeat in your toes every time I touch you. But I won't pretend for you."

He takes a deep breath, and when he lets it out, a waft of mint greets my nose.

"This is happening, Fallon. Open your eyes," he growls out.

But I can't.

He lets go, leaving a chill in his wake. I finally open my eyes, searching the room until I find his retreating figure pushing through a set of doors. It takes me a moment to adjust to my surroundings again, and when I do, I look around and find that everyone on the dance floor is staring at me. They've all stopped dancing. They all share the same shocked expression. I realize Jesse knew very well that he was telling the entire school how he felt about me. But what I find even more shocking is the urge I feel to run after him. My feet begin to move before my brain can catch up with the idea of chasing after him, but I'm not fast enough in these shoes. I yank them off and run on my bare feet, leaving my shoes on the floor like Cinderella. I shove the doors open, bursting into the hallway. It's empty; no Jesse in sight. I decide to check a few of the places I thought he would go to. I turn to begin running again, but hands slam into my back and push me into the wall of lockers. It happens so quickly I'm not sure what's going on. I turn my head to look, but I hear his slimy voice instead.

"How sweet. You're running after him like a sad, pathetic, little puppy."

"Marcus?" Fear has me frozen in place. "What are you doing here?" I whisper.

"A little birdie told me you were going to be at a dance in a pretty dress." His sing-song voice washes over me as he slides his hand down my side. The contents of my stomach roil and begin to rise at his touch. I take deep, even breaths, hoping it will push down some of the panic I feel at being alone with him again. I squirm, trying to pull out of his grasp, but it's no use.

I hear a rumble in his chest, and I close my eyes, praying someone comes into this hallway.

"It is quite hilarious that you think you can put up a fight. He must have really boosted your confidence."

Marcus yanks me back and turns around, leaving a space between us that is just big enough for me to push my flat palm as hard as I can into his nose.

"You bitch!" He grabs his face, and blood is already pouring out of his nose.

I run for it, trying to put distance between us, but he grabs me. In the back of my mind, I register the sound of something ripping.

He slams me back into the lockers. I hit something hard, and pain radiates down my back into my legs. I cry out as my eyes become moist, but I refuse to give him any more of my tears. He pushes his chest against me, trapping my legs and holding my arms above my head, keeping me in place.

He pushes even closer; his pupils are so dilated that they remind me of a black hole. They suck you in and never let you leave. I turn my head away from him and stretch as far from him as I can. Closing my eyes, I try to focus on calming myself enough to figure out how to get out of this. I refuse to let him win again.

"You need to remember who you are dealing with," he growls.

He quickly grabs my chin and yanks it towards him. He lifts me higher until I'm nearly standing on the tips of my toes. Grabbing at my breast, he leans in and licks my earlobe before hissing, "You will always be mine."

And then he's suddenly pulled from me, and I'm free of his hold. I faintly register a loud bang and his body comes into view on the ground before me.

"You son of a bitch. I'll kill you," an angry growl vibrates through the air, filling me with sweet relief.

Jesse.

I sink down the wall and flop onto the floor. I watch as Jesse jumps on Marcus, sitting on his chest. He hits him over and over. After what seems like forever, people run out to the hallway looking for the source of the noise. Someone touches my arm, and I try to focus on the face. Jade comes in and out of focus as I strain to look at her. Her lips are moving, but I can't quite figure out what she's saying.

What's that ringing?

I sense him before I feel him as I'm lifted into his strong arms. I grab ahold of the collar of his shirt and breathe in his cologne.

I'm safe.

With the feeling of safety running through me, the weight of reality comes crashing over me, and I feel the sting of tears forming. Before I know it, a sob falls out of me.

I almost fell victim to him again.

169

"Shhh, you're okay, baby. You're safe." Jesse's gentle voice makes it to my ears, and it causes the sobs to come harder.

CHAPTER TWENTY-NINE

I remain in Jesse's arms as he puts us in the back seat of a car. I vaguely remember the car stopping and him bringing me through a door. He puts me down on something hard, and I blink, realizing we are no longer in the school gym. I look down at his bathroom counter under me. I lift my eyes and watch him turn the shower on. Whorls of steam start to rise up. He steps out of the bathroom and comes back a few moments later with clothes in his hand that he lays next to me on the counter.

"Here, let me help you with that." He points to my dress, and I look down at the ripped fabric. My bra has been on display for everyone to see. I nod for him to go ahead.

Damn it. I really loved this dress.

He gently brings me down from the counter, and I give him my back. He tries to unzip the dress, but the damage makes it impossible to undo.

"I'm going to have to rip it. Okay?" He murmurs the question into my ear as goosebumps form on my arms.

"Okay," I say. My voice cracks.

He yanks on the fabric, and I feel it give. Cool air slides across my back, causing a chill, and his hand sweeps up and down my arms.

"I'll be right outside if you need me." His hand starts slipping away, and I quickly place mine over it, gripping his hard.

"Jesse?" I turn to him, meeting his gaze, baring everything I'm feeling so he can see it.

"I'm here." His voice wraps around my body like a warm cocoon. He steps close to me, wrapping one hand around my waist as he looks into my eyes and pushes my hair back from my face with his other hand.

"Please don't go." I swallow.

"Fallon . . ." He hesitates while he studies me. He brings his palm to my face, and I turn into it, closing my eyes, breathing in the comfort his touch gives me.

"I need you to erase it. Him. His touch," I say.

I open my eyes, look directly into his, and bring my hands up to the torn straps of my dress. I slowly lower them, my stare unwavering. He swallows thickly, his gaze following the material until it hits the floor. He slowly takes in my body inch by inch, studying each curve. As his gaze lifts to mine, warmth spreads through my legs rising into my stomach as the licks of burning need scald me from the inside. I raise a shaky hand to unhook my bra, but he stops me. He turns me around so that my back is to him.

"Shit," he hisses, and I know he's looking at the bruises I feel already forming from the lockers. He kneels down, grasping both sides of my hips. "I'm so sorry, Fallon."

He gently guides his lips up the length of my spine. My fingers are tingling by the time he makes it to my shoulders. He stands up, slowly sliding his hands up my sides. He places a kiss on my shoulder as my bra falls away leaving me in nothing but my underwear.

I turn to face him, every part of me on edge from need for him. My heartbeat pulses down my arms into my hands. My gaze stays low, avoiding his expression when he finds me utterly bare to him, body and soul. His knuckle nudges my chin, bringing my eyes up to meet his. My breath catches in my throat. His dilated pupils are ignited with desire.

"Keep your eyes on me, Fallon."

Jesse steps back to pull his shirt over his head, throwing it off to the side. He reaches for the buttons on his jeans and slowly pulls them down, stepping out of them completely. My nostrils flare as my breathing becomes erratic. I take in his glorious body. I follow every line on his stomach down to his prominent V, silently appreciating his love for a sport.

He stalks towards me with hooded eyes and grips me by my thighs, quickly lifting me. My legs wrap around his waist as his gaze turns from burning to hungry. With my arms loosely draped around his neck, he steps into the shower. The heat from the water hits my back as he guides us directly into the stream. He opens the shampoo bottle and lifts it to my head where he squirts it directly onto my hair. His free hand runs through it all, working the shampoo in, with the other hand still gripping my thigh. He grabs a puff and hands it to me as he brings his musky bodywash to it. It's the same musky scent he wears every day, the one that drives me wild.

Swiping the puff across my chest and down my sides, Jesse scrubs hard. He's trying to erase as much as he can before he replaces it with his own touch. Neither of us breaks eye contact as he takes his time with me, but I know it's taking everything in him to hold himself back. He's rock-hard against my soaked underwear. He puts the soap down once he has scrubbed every inch he could reach. Finally convinced I'm clean, he lets the water run over us, rinsing away the soap and the feel of Marcus' hands on me down the drain. I tighten my legs around his waist so I can lean my head into the water. I close my eyes and enjoy the feel of it running over me, bringing my hands to my hair.

"You are so fucking beautiful." A deep grumble comes from his chest.

I bring my head back and open my eyes. His control is faltering, and struggle lines his face. He needs me just as much as I need him. I grip the back of his neck as both of his hands grip me, pulling me closer to his arousal.

"I can't wait anymore." His gruff voice echoes through the shower as he guides my lips down, plunging his tongue into my mouth in an urgent kiss. He props me against the shower wall so he can rub his hands up my body and over my breasts, lightly kneading them. He pushes his hardness against me, and I gasp, bucking my hips into him. His lips trail down my chin to my neck and stop on my shoulder; his hands tease my nipples and make my need for him to be inside me become too much.

"Jesse, please," I plead.

He growls and reaches down between us, rubbing against my sweet spot, making me squirm under his touch until he wraps a finger around my panties, ripping them from me. He lifts me by the ass to line up with me. His jaw tightens, and he stops to look at me under pinched eyebrows.

"Are you sure? Once we go here, there is no going back. You're mine. Do you understand?" His piercing eyes captivate me, and I realize right then that there was never a question; I was always his. It just took me a while to figure it out.

Instead of answering him, I push myself down on him until he thrusts up, filling me perfectly. He moans and places his head on my shoulder as he shudders, letting me adjust to him.

He stills. "Condom?"

"I'm on birth control." I say.

"Baby," his breathy voice glides over me as he begins to thrust into me.

"You're mine too . . ." My voice is so raspy I'm not sure it belongs to me.

His head snaps up, and his nostrils flare. He studies me for a moment. I let him see everything. My fear, my want, and my trust. I reach up, slide my hands onto the nape of his neck, and I pull, commanding his lips to mine. He nudges my mouth open with his tongue joining mine, our mouths in a fervent dance. This winds him up, and he releases a growl that vibrates through his chest. He pulls back, stilling himself, then abruptly slams back into me over and over.

The feeling is almost too much. I close my eyes and drop my head back, panting as pressure builds inside of me. He grabs my chin, bringing my head down to his, and I open my heavy eyes to meet his.

"Keep your eyes on me," he growls, keeping his pace.

Jesse's words excite me. He wants to see me come undone for him. As the pressure builds, I fight the urge to close my eyes. My walls clench down, anticipating my release. His jaw tightens, trying to keep his control; he's not too far behind me. The pressure builds in my core and down my legs, teetering on the edge. He rocks into me one last time and hits my back wall, holding it. That one move pushes me over so hard tears form as it spreads through me. I moan his name as my entire body is consumed by the explosion. My walls pulse around him as my stomach tightens, and all I can do is ride it out. He slowly thrusts into me, dragging out my orgasm until his entire body shudders with his release. He presses his lips into a slow kiss with each tremble pushing us closer until we're both spent.

I try to control my breathing as I sag against him, his hand bracing us against the wall. He pulls back, reaching around to turn the water off. I feel a blast of cold air as he carries me out of the shower. He gently rubs his hand down my back, giving me chills. I lift my head, my need for him growing again. He swears and deposits me on his bed, lowering his hard body over me. This is how we stay for the rest of the night, claiming each other over and over again with our kisses and our bodies and our words. We are no longer fighting our feelings; instead, for this one night, we are living in them.

CHAPTER THIRTY

I stir to the sound of a crash. It doesn't take much to realize it's the bedroom door slamming into the wall. Jesse jumps up, immediately blocking me from whoever is coming through the door.

"Get your ass out of bed son!" a voice booms across the room.

"Dad? What the hell are you doing? Get out!" Jesse yells.

His dad. I'm naked in his son's bed, and this is how I meet him for the first time.

I do a mental facepalm. This can't be good.

"Oh, isn't that great," he sneers when he sees me. "Get dressed and meet me in the office. NOW." He turns to walk out but stops a few steps short of the door. Turning over his shoulder, he sneers, "And get that girl out of here."

Jesse jumps up quickly, rushes over to his closet and throws on whatever he reaches first. He skips brushing his teeth and goes straight for mouthwash. I sit still watching him.

Cason comes rushing through the door.

"Dude, what is going on? Your dad just called a meeting?" Cason stops short, finally realizing I'm in bed with the sheets pulled up. He brings his hand up quickly to cover his eyes.

"Sorry, Fallon, I didn't know. I mean, thank fuck you guys figured this shit out." Cason drops his hand to stare at Jesse, who is now fully clothed and leaning against the bathroom door frame with his arms crossed and biceps bulging. He's pulled on a black V-neck with jeans that sit low on his hips. My mouth is suddenly watering.

"It's Marcus. I'm sure he got word of our run-in last night," Jesse says, staring at me. And suddenly I'm angry. Angry at myself for letting this happen. None of this should have happened.

"So what? You're in trouble with daddy now for protecting me?" I sneer. "Sorry, I didn't mean to be a problem."

I drop the blanket and stand grabbing my clothes. My body is on full display for both Jesse and Cason.

"Cason. Leave," Jesse says as I pull on my clothes.

Cason looks between us before quickly walking out of the room, closing the door behind him. I roll my eyes at Jesse's display of dominance.

"Fallon," he says, as I pull on my shirt and reach for my shoes. I am pointedly ignoring him. "Fallon," he says much more firmly. When I ignore him again, he moves to stand in front of me. "Look at me, dammit." He grinds his teeth.

"Do not do that. I'm not one of your little minions that run around here doing whatever you say," I snap. Tears begin to run down my face.

His eyes widen a bit, but he quickly recovers. He chuckles then. "No, you are most definitely not." Jesse shakes his head, but the amusement quickly fades to something darker and more serious. "You are so much more than that. What happened to you last night was not your fault."

He clenches his jaw, causing the muscles to flex. He reaches for me, bends down to be at my level and stare directly into my eyes. "I shouldn't have left you alone like that. I should've . . . I won't make that mistake again."

If I could see into his soul right now, I know it would be dark and swirling. He doesn't blame me or my past for bringing this into his world.

I meet his eyes. His walls are down. He's giving me everything. No masks, and no hiding. This is him, and I can see the want, need, anger, fear, and worst of all: guilt.

"No way. If you aren't going to let me blame myself, then you don't get to sit here and try to convince me it was your fault either."

A sigh comes out as emotional exhaustion hits me square in the chest.

"We're going to have to deal with him, aren't we?" I have been running from Marcus for so long that I wasn't sure I knew any other way besides fear. Last night was the first time I fought back, and I'm not so sure it isn't because of Jesse that I had that strength.

Jesse and I go downstairs together for his meeting with his father. He brings me to the kitchen where his mother is sitting at the counter drinking coffee. When she looks up, I notice the puffiness under her eyes and dark circles immediately. I can see the worry lines etched through her face, yet she still holds a loving smile for her son.

"Hey, Ma," Jesse says before sweeping down and giving her a kiss on the cheek.

"Take good care of her," he whispers loud enough for me to hear. He straightens with an arrogant smile and a wink of the eye. He gives me my own kiss to the temple before walking out to go meet his father.

His mother watches him go, and I see the lines become deeper in the ten seconds her eyes follow him.

"Would you like something to drink? The boys keep water and those sports drinks around. I also have the good coffee hiding away if you would like that, but you have to promise not to share with my kids. They're like vultures. They'll drink me dry." She laughs.

"Your secret is safe with me. Coffee would be nice." I smile up at her as she makes her way to the coffee pot.

"Cream or sugar?" she asks without turning around.

"Cream, please. A lot." I reply and she chuckles.

After a minute or two, Catherine sets a mug down in front of me with steaming coffee in it. The moment the scent touches my nose, I'm drooling. She watches me for a moment and chews on her lip. Something's on her mind, and I watch her go through a range of emotions as I sip on the warm coffee.

"Fallon, can I ask you something?" She looks at me with eyes full of sorrow. It surprises me since she seems to be a genuinely happy person.

"Uh, sure. Go ahead." I put the mug down. I really wanted to finish this cup of coffee, but luck doesn't appear to be on my side this morning.

"Is Jesse happy? It's just . . . I worry about him because we're gone a lot, and his father puts so much pressure on him. I just want to know he's happy." I see a sheen over her eyes as she holds back tears for her baby. I contemplate how to answer her for a minute. I don't know what to say.

"I think so . . . I haven't really known him long enough to say," I tell her. I'm not entirely honest with my answer, and she knows it, because she quickly calls me out on it.

Damn Mother's intuition.

"But? There is something you aren't telling me, honey. It's written all over your face."

I sigh. "This stuff with his father. He doesn't get to be a kid in high school. His every move is calculated, and he never lets his guard down. He is always trying to make that man proud, and it never seems to be enough. I don't think he will ever be happy if he continues to strive for his dad and not for himself."

She stares at me for a long moment. "I see why he likes you." She gives me a smirk before she picks up our cups and brings them to the sink.

"I'm going to use the restroom," I say as I get up and move towards the door.

"He trusts you. I haven't seen him trust anyone besides his siblings. But you? He looks at you with pure adoration, and you look at him with the same. But with you, it's masked with fear."

I stop at the threshold as she speaks, and her words really hit me in the gut. The air is smacked out of me. I manage to move my feet and keep walking until I get to the hall, where I lean against the wall to catch my breath. She's right. I do fear everything I feel for him. Last night has only made that feeling stronger.

Unexpectedly, I hear shouting. "It's that girl! You brought her here, and now I have to clean up your mess. Get rid of her Jesse, before she causes more problems." I realize I'm standing next to his father's office.

"Ain't happenin'." Jesse's voice sweeps through, and I hear the firmness in his tone.

"Dammit Jesse! What if he pressed charges against you? Are you going to throw your life away for some trailer trash looking for a free ride?"

I flinch at his words, and before I know it, I'm running out the front door. I vaguely hear someone calling after me, but I don't care. I'm on emotional overload and need to get away. I keep pushing my legs until they have nothing left to give me, and then I continue walking.

I keep going, and when I finally do stop, I have no idea how I ended up this far away, but there is no way I can walk back. I don't really even know where I am. I feel my panic rising in my throat.

I'm a stupid girl.

I keep walking along the sidewalks in front of businesses I have never seen before until I find a bus stop. I sit on the dirty green bench that the city provides. My butt barely hits the grate before a sob comes up. I lay on my side, pulling my feet to tuck behind me and let the tears fall freely until there are none left.

"Fallon!"

I think I hear my name being called, but I'm not sure where the voice is coming from. *It's just a dream.*

"Fallon, baby, please."

I hear the pleading in the familiar voice. That sounds a little too loud to be in my dream. A hand touches my shoulder and shakes me gently.

Definitely not a dream.

I open my eyes, and they widen a bit at the startled realization that Jesse is kneeling in front of me.

"Jesse?" I ask, confusion lacing my voice.

Why is he here? Where is here?

"Jesus Fallon, we have been looking all over for you. Are you ok? What happened?" He helps me up into a sitting position as I start taking in my surroundings.

I'm at a bus stop . . .

The conversation with Jesse's mom, my panic, Jesse's dad, Jesse's future . . . I remember it all now.

"Fallon, say something!" I look up at him. He's frustrated—evident in the way he holds his mouth in a thin straight line—but I know in my gut that frustration stems from worry for me.

He's worried about me.

"I'm fine." I bring my hand to my temple as a pounding pulses across my forehead and through my eyes.

"You're fine? That's why I just found you sleeping on a bus stop bench?" The sarcasm is dripping from his voice, and his anger is taking over the worry. He stands up and turns around, taking a few steps away from me. He brings his hand up to run through his hair before turning back to me.

"Fallon, do you know how fucking worried I was about you? I mean you just left. You just disappeared. You can't do this kind of shit anymore, not now. Not after last night." I watch his tense body shake. I hear his words, but do they really matter?

Obviously, I wasn't thinking all that clearly when I stormed out, but I just needed a moment to filter through the emotions invading my mind.

"He's right, you know." I don't want his dad to be right. But underneath it all, I know he is.

"Who?" Jesse looks back to me with one eyebrow cocked, throwing his hands up in the air. "Who's right?"

"Your dad. You could have been arrested because of me. Your future could have been ruined. I can't be the reason you don't have a future."

Jesse freezes when I mention his dad.

"I overheard you and your dad when I was going to the restroom. I didn't mean to. It just happened. But I can't disagree with some of it, and I didn't mean to worry you. I got lost, and I didn't have a phone."

Jesse sits on the bench next to me, bracing his elbows on his knees. He rubs his hands down his face. He's tired; I see the bags under his eyes. The crow's feet he shouldn't even have at his age are more prominent today.

"Fallon, I would have thought you'd have figured it out by now, but since you need me to say it, here it is: you were going to be mine from the first moment you fell into me. I don't care what that man says or what's in our pasts. What I do know is nothing would have kept me away from you. Not Marcus, not this screwed up life we were both given, and especially not my father. I know you feel the same way, but you need to accept that for yourself—I can't do it for you." He rubs the side of his face once more before he stands. "Hell, pushing you to see it only makes you want to run away more. At some point, you will have to stop running away from the people who care about you." He pauses. "My life would be damn lonely without you in it."

I snap my head up to him, but he has already turned away and is walking to his car parked on the curb. My head is heavy, I'm hungry, and Jesse just sent my mind into shock—not that it's a hard thing to do right now. I hear the rumble of his engine starting and look through the windshield to the driver's side, where he is watching me, patiently waiting for me.

I don't deserve him. I don't deserve a man that is willing to hold me up when I crumble at my own faults.

I stand, making up my mind right then. I want to be the person he needs. I want to trust in him, in us. But most importantly, I want to fight for it. He makes me want to fight for it.

I join him in his car and lean over as soon as I'm settled in, before he can put his car in drive. I kiss him like my life depends on his touch. I pull him as close to me as possible. I feel like I'm skydiving and he's my parachute. I finally pull back, my breathing coming fast with our foreheads touching. My hands caging each side of his face.

"Okay." I say between heavy breaths. "I heard you."

"Are you sure?" He pulls back and looks me over, searching my face to see if there is any hint of hesitation or doubt. I don't have any, so he doesn't find any, and he nods, satisfied with what he sees. He brings his forehead back to mine and lets out a quick breath in relief. "Thank fuck. I can't do this without you."

He gives me a small peck on the lips before pulling away to put the car in drive. His hand finds mine, he tangles our fingers together, and it feels good. His firm grip gives me strength in ways I didn't know I needed.

CHAPTER THIRTY-ONE

Jade comes bouncing into my room as her usual chipper self. I'm towel-drying my hair after a hot shower with her brother. Thankfully, he went back to his room to get dressed for school. I haven't exactly told her about our newfound relationship. I don't think Cason would share the news, since Jesse all but told him to forget what he saw.

"So, I was thinking . . ." Jade lays across my bed, staring at me. I turn towards her quickly.

"This can't be good," I mumble to myself.

"I heard that." She frowns at me.

"You were supposed to." I give her a little chuckle.

"So, the boys are working with Dad tonight. I thought maybe we could go out, just us," she says. She pulls a pillow in and hugs it. I realize I haven't spent a lot of time with her in the last few days. With everything that has happened, I just haven't found the time.

"I don't know, Jade. Your brother is pretty adamant that I not go anywhere without him."

Jade snorts at this. "Oh, come on, Fallon. He isn't going to be here. Since when do you listen to him anyway?"

She throws the pillow at me, and I duck, laughing with her.

"Okay, okay! What do you have in mind?" I ask. Jade always has something up her sleeve.

"Well, Miranda Stevens invited a bunch of us over to her house to hang out and get ready. Then I think they were going over to the Depot."

I've seen Miranda around the school and at a few parties. She's on the dance team, but she seems nice enough. Maybe I could tell Jesse to meet us over at the Depot when they get done? I'll have to talk to him about it.

"Yeah, okay. I think it could be fun. I just have to stop by the hospital to check on my mom first."

Jade squeals a bit. "Okay! It'll be so much fun. I finally get you to myself." She gets up. "I have to go text Miranda to let her know. I'll see you downstairs."

I laugh as Jade runs out of the room and nearly collides with Jesse. He moves out of the way just in time.

"Woah! Jade, watch where you're going," he hollers after her.

He leans on the door frame watching me. "What's with her?"

I shake my head, still chuckling. "She's just excited. A bunch of girls are meeting up tonight before heading over the Depot. She wants me to go."

"Fallon . . ." Jesse starts, and I know what's coming, so I hold my hand up.

"Jesse, don't. I haven't spent a lot of time with Jade lately, and it's just the Depot. You can't be everywhere all of the time. Besides, Jade will be there, and I'll be with a group."

He takes a step into my room and shuts the door behind him. I swallow hard because I can't tell if he's upset or not. He stalks toward me, and I step backwards until I hit my dresser. He leans in, placing a hand on each side of me, caging me in.

"Fine. You can go. But you need to stay with the group, and you call me if any of Jax's guys show up."

"I will. Do you think you and Cason will be done early enough to meet us?"

"I honestly don't know. Dad hasn't really told us what this is about." He makes a face that tells me he doesn't like being in the dark like this. It gives me the impression that his dad doesn't usually withhold information from him.

I drop my head to his chest, breathing in a hint of his body wash. His arms wrap around me, and I look up at him lazily.

He kisses me slowly and I lose myself in him, in his touch, in the feel of his lips on mine. He's attentive to what my body wants from him. I encircle my arms around his neck and bring him closer. Our usual sizzle is there, but there's something else in this kiss. It's comforting and calming. His lips are my solace.

He pulls back slightly but rests his forehead to mine. "Please be careful tonight." He straightens as he grabs my chin, tilting my head to look up at him. I try very hard not to roll my eyes, but I fail. "I'm serious, Fallon. I need to be able to focus tonight, and I won't be able to do that if I'm worried about you."

"I'll be fine, Jess. I promise. If anything goes down, you'll be the first person I call."

He looks at me for a moment. I know he really doesn't like this, but I let him know without words that I'm taking this seriously. He leans down and meets my lips with another chaste kiss before letting me go.

"Come on, babe. We need to get going." Just as he says that, the horn that I determine is coming from his car rings through the walls.

We both look at each other and simultaneously huff out, "Jade." Jesse laughs before grabbing my hand. He leads us to his car, and my heart warms as I think about how much I would like this morning to be our normal.

We pull up at school, and Jesse parks in his usual spot. I have come to the conclusion that avoiding being seen doesn't work when you are getting out of Jesse Callaway's car, so I gave up and started joining them as they congregate in the rear parking lot. Jade and I walk over to a few of the guy's girlfriends. Jade starts discussing tonight with them. I lean against a nearby tailgate that a few of the guys, including Jordan, are sitting on.

"Hey, Fallon. I hear you guys are going to the Depot tonight," Jordan says.

"That seems to be the plan," I tell him as Jade's voice carries over to me, full of excitement.

"Cool, I'm going with a few of the guys too. The races are supposed to be lit tonight."

He smiles at me, but a tingling in my neck has me looking for Jesse. I find him a few feet away, glaring in Jordan's direction. I knit my eyebrows together and tilt my head asking him what's wrong. His eyes find mine, and his face softens. With a shake of his head, he gives me a small half-smile. The first bell rings, and we all start making our way into the school. I grab my books out of my locker and quickly go to homeroom. I spot Jesse leaning against the wall next to the door of our class. As I draw near, he pushes off the wall to meet me. Something is bothering him. I can see it in the way his eyebrows are wrinkled and his mouth is stretched into a tight line.

"Hey. What is it?" I reach up to smooth his brow out with my fingertip.

He closes his eyes for a moment, reveling in my touch before reaching up to grab my hand.

When his eyes open, whatever is bothering him seems to ease. He takes no time to pull me into our classroom. "Come on, let's go in."

By the time lunch comes around, I've forgotten about Jesse's uneasiness. I go straight for the line to grab lunch and head to our usual spot in the quad on our picnic table. Except when I get closer, I find Elizabeth sitting on the table, pom-poms in hand, with her feet nearly touching Jesse as he leans away from her towering body. She laughs at something he says and he tenses. The red haze of jealousy catches me off guard. I didn't even realize that is an emotion I'm capable of. My feet stop moving at some point, and I just stand there watching them together.

Jesse looks up in my direction, like he knew my eyes are on him. He narrows his eyes, questioning me. But when he glances at Elizabeth and then back to me, they widen, the reason why I'm not moving any closer finally dawning on him. He watches me, waiting, and effectively ignoring Elizabeth. He cocks his head to the side, almost asking for me. I can tell in the way his eyes tighten that he wants to know what I'm going to do. He's questioning if I'm really his or not. If he's mine. If I'm really in this with him.

Shit.

Elizabeth takes this moment to rub her hand down Jesse's arm.

What game does she think she is playing at? Fuck this. He's mine.

People still as I start walking again towards my man in an almost predatory fashion. Elizabeth's back is turned to me. She's none the wiser about what's coming for her. My gait doesn't falter, and neither do my eyes as they stay locked onto Jesse's. I can tell he knows what is coming by the smirk on his face, but there is something else deep in his gaze. A burning need for me. I don't hesitate as I forcibly wedge my body between them, knocking Elizabeth off the table. I'm vaguely aware of her yelling, but I couldn't care less. Jesse leans back, making room for me as I straddle him and immediately pull his lips to mine. This kiss is different than any previous public kiss, though. This time, we're claiming each other for all to see. I've commandeered everyone's attention, and my mouth is taking ownership of the man that sits beneath me. But he and I both know this kiss is about more than Elizabeth.

"You heard me." His scorching gaze is fixated on me and has me captured, unable to move. The fear I usually feel isn't present. It's been replaced with a thirst for more of this man.

"I heard you. I'm here." Lost in his eyes, I'm unaware of the attention I've garnered with this move.

"Holy. Shit. When the fuck? Why the fuck? Why didn't you tell me?" Jade's voice is heard screeching over my shoulder. I wince as I come back to reality, well aware that most of the school is watching us. I go to move, but Jesse doesn't let me go, so I turn towards the table, his hands holding me by the thighs. I lean against him, using his shoulder to rest my head.

"Oh, please. Get a room." This comes from Elizabeth as she dusts her butt off and storms away. I'd honestly forgotten she was there.

I laugh at her retreating figure while Cason roars out, "You just melted the ice queen into a puddle of mud, literally." The entire table has joined in on the fun. A deep rumble vibrates behind me, and I turn to meet Jesse's smiling face. My breath hitches at this beautiful man, and I feel overjoyed that he has allowed himself to take a moment of happiness without guilt or worry. My own smile meets his, and with a wink, he tells me without words that he feels the shift too.

189

CHAPTER THIRTY-TWO

After spending two hours picking out the perfect outfit and making sure our hair and make-up were "on point," as Jade called it, we have finally arrived at Miranda Stevens' place. I roll my eyes at the two-story house that has mansion-like qualities, like wrought-iron balconies and custom shutters.

Of course, every person on this side of town is rolling in money.

I told Jade I'd rather get dressed at our house, so we're just picking them up. Three girls walk out the front door and greet us. Miranda is leading the pack. We borrowed Cason's Jeep since they took Jesse's car to go do whatever it is they're doing. As we watch them head toward our car, it occurs to me that Jade doesn't have her own vehicle.

"Why do the boys have vehicles, and not you?" I ask Jade.

"Oh, I decided that I would much prefer to have my brother to chauffeur me around town than have my own ride." I give her a pointed look to tell her I didn't believe that.

"Ok, so I may have failed my driver's test a few times, and the parents thought it would be best if we waited to buy a car for me."

"How many times?"

"Hm?"

"Your driver's test, Jade. How many times did you fail?"

The back door of the passenger side is pulled open, and the girls pile in. Jade smiles in my direction as I glare at her. This conversation isn't over.

The Depot is so packed I begin to question whether or not this was a good idea after all. When Jade pulls into the lot, the crowd parts for us just like they do for Jesse, allowing us front-row parking.

We all file out and head straight for the guys on the basketball team. I feel a little better being surrounded by Jesse's boys in a crowd like this. It doesn't take long before a beer is passed to me. I accept it, but only sip on it. I don't feel comfortable drinking around people I don't know, especially without Jesse here.

When did I start relying on Jesse so much?

"Hey there, pretty, what is your name?" A dirty blonde guy that smelled of something more than beer stumbled over to me.

"Be careful there, Zac. That's Jesse's girl," a familiar voice says from behind me. When I turn around, I find Jordan.

"Hey man, you racing tonight?" Zac shuffles over to Jordan to give him a sloppy bro hug.

"You know it." Jordan slaps Zac on the shoulder then nudges him away from me. "I think that girl over there is looking at you. You should go get her number." Jordan points at a blonde chick about twenty yards away that hasn't glanced in this direction once.

"You think so, man? Ooohh yeah, imma hit that tonight." Zac stumbles off towards the girl. I shake my head after him and snort.

More like she's gonna hit you.

"Yo, Jesse's girl, you enjoying the races tonight?" Jordan nods to the track.

"You know my name, Jordan. And they're alright. I haven't seen anything that exciting so far." I shrug my shoulders.

"That's because you haven't seen me race yet." His eyes lift up, and he smirks at me. *This cocky bastard sure thinks he is something, alright.*

"What makes you so special?" I ask, curiosity getting the best of me.

"The second flag up there. The one that has my name on it. Says I'm undefeated, and that makes me kind of special out here." He lifts his hands and turns his upper body left and right.

And he only gets cockier.

"Boy, you need to open your eyes and check that first flag, 'cause there is still one person you haven't beat." Shady's raspy voice has my head turning in her direction, but I smelled her stale cigarettes before she spoke.

"But where is he, Shady? It's hard to beat someone that doesn't come out here anymore." He's still smiling, but there is a glimmer of something in his eyes. Jealousy, maybe?

Shady shakes her head while laughing. "You know he's busy. But if he ever does get back out here, he could sure show you a thing or two."

I want to know who they are talking about, so I look up at the first flag. It reads: *Jesse Callaway.*

"I knew Jesse raced, but I didn't know he was good," I murmur to myself more than anything.

"Oh yeah, he was one of the best out here. I've never seen anyone else behind the wheel with that much control." Shady's eyes blank out for a second, remembering young Jesse racing. "Family duties called, and this one showed up, keeping the cash flow coming."

"Say Jesse's girl, you ever raced before?"

"Nope. I don't even have a license yet."

"Like that matters," Shady snorts

"My race is up next. You wanna ride?" Jordan is smiling at me.

"Jordan, stop stirring up trouble. You know damn well he doesn't want her on that track." Shady turns to me, shaking her head while putting a cigarette to her lips and lighting it. "He asked me to keep an eye out for you, and if Jesse finds out I let you race? Well, he won't be too happy."

"Wait. He asked you to babysit me?" Something about him asking Shady to look after me when I suspect he used to *look after her* really doesn't sit well with me.

"Ah shit, girl. It isn't like that. He's just worried about you," she tells me out of the corner of her mouth, the cigarette hanging out the other side.

"Come on, Shady, she's a big girl. She can make her own decisions."

I probably should walk away, but something about the way that Jesse went behind me to have his ex . . . thing . . . watch me has my blood boiling. Before I can stop myself, I'm already asking. I narrow my eyes at Shady, and I see a glint of humor in hers.

"Jordan?" I ask.

"Yeah?"

"I think I might just ride after all." I turn to him, and his smile is bright, lighting up his face like I'd just given him his favorite candy.

"Alright, come on, let's do this!" Jordan shouts as he makes his way to a blue mustang parked not far from us. It's a pretty car, but it isn't nearly as pretty as Jesse's.

Shady chuckles. "I see why he likes you. You're a stubborn one— I bet you give him all kinds of trouble."

I watch Shady walk off before heading to the passenger side of Jordan's car.

As I open the door, I hear someone call my name. I look around until my eyes land on Jade's.

"What are you doing Fallon? Jesse will kill you!" Jade shouts to me as she tries to push herself through the crowd. I hurriedly drop myself into the passenger seat and shut the door.

"Go, before they yank me out of this car," I tell Jordan. He smiles and puts the car in gear.

Jordan lines up on the starting line of the track. A little red Honda Civic is already there waiting. With the sound of the muffler and the look of the Civic, the owner has done some serious modifications. I'm not sure if they help the car move any faster, though.

Jordan revs his engine a few times as a girl in a bikini and jean shorts saunters out in front of us and stands in between the two cars. She has a flag in her hand.

Her lips are moving. She's speaking to the crowd, and I think I catch, "On your mark," but before I can finish reading her lips, the flag drops and Jordan hits the gas. The track we're on is a straight stretch for about a quarter of a mile. Whoever makes it to the finish line first wins the race. And that finish line is coming up fast, but at the same time, it isn't. My heart is racing at about the same mph the car is going. The exhilaration of the speed has my mind focused solely on me. Time is standing still, and all that matters is that I'm flying.

"Jordan, he's pulling ahead," I shout over the sound of the motor.

"Don't worry, he won't be for long," Jordan tells me just as he presses the gas pedal a little harder. And we're flying higher. I'm soaring down a dirt track, but I'm way up in the clouds.

We near the finish line, and right before we cross over it, Jordan is able to pull just a bumper's width ahead. That's enough to win the race. He slows down and pulls to a stop. Before we're even able to get out of the car, a crowd of people surround us. Jordan jumps out smiling. One girl walks up straight up to him and gives him the sloppiest kiss I have ever seen. I slowly exit the vehicle, dreading the shit I know I'm going to get for this.

"Fallon! Are you *crazy*? Jesse is going to be so mad at you! He is never going to let us hang out again!" Jade screams as she launches herself at me.

"Jade, I'm okay. Besides, Jesse can't tell me what to do."

"I bet you won't be saying that in about five minutes when lover-boy shows up," Shady interrupts.

I snap my head up and glare at her. I know she did not call him.

"You called him?" I snip out.

"Honey, I wouldn't be on his daddy's payroll if it wasn't for that boy. I let you get in that car but don't for one second think I wasn't going to tell him. It's nothing personal, it's just business."

Jade steps forward this time.

"Did you forget there's a Callaway out here? You are out of line, Shady," Jade growls. I'm proud of Jade; she's empowering me to stand tall. She's holding her family's name with a commanding presence.

"Oh please, baby Callaway, we both know Daddy won't listen to you. But Jesse? Well, he holds all of the power."

Tires squeal, making us all look up as a black Camaro drifts to a halt. Jesse is out of the car and storming in my direction before I can blink. His brows furrow, and his hand makes a fist. He's pissed.

Oh shit. This is so not good.

But instead of coming to me, he rounds on Jordan, slamming him into the side of his car, pushing his forearm against Jordan's throat.

"What the fuck you think you're doing?" Jesse snarls out. Jordan throws his hands up.

"She's a big girl, Callaway. She can make her own decisions," Jordan throws back at him.

Jesse pushes his arm a little harder. By the way Jordan's face is turning red, he's struggling to breathe.

I rush over, placing my hand on Jesse's bicep. "Jesse, let him go. This isn't his fault. I got in his car on my own."

"That's right, Callaway, run off with your girl. Not like you care about us little people anymore, anyway," Jordan says, and I narrow my eyes at him.

What is he getting at? I thought they are friends.

I pull on Jesse again, and his eyes slice to mine. He isn't done yet. His next victim is likely going to be me.

He grinds his teeth a little before releasing Jordan. But turns back to him, lowering his eyes, his lip turns up snarling, "You better watch yourself."

He walks off, heading back to his car with Cason in tow. When I don't fall in line, Cason turns back to me. I can see it. A pleading look crosses over his face, asking me to not force his hand here.

I let out a sigh and get my feet into gear, deciding to humor him.

The ride home is silent. No one says a word, there is no music, and Cason has no jokes. I bounce my leg out of nervous habit.

We finally get home, and Jesse goes straight to his room. I wasn't prepared to fight with him tonight, so I slip into my room and change into my sleep clothes. I flop out onto the bed and stare up at the ceiling, knowing as long as Jesse stays in his room I won't be sleeping. I decide to attempt it anyway, having nothing else to do, and reach over to turn the lamp off. I slide under the covers. After about an hour of lying there, I hear the doorknob turn and light peaks across the bed onto the wall. With my back to the door, I can't see who it is, but I don't have to turn around to know. The bed dips as he slides in, pulling me to him. My back hits his hard chest, and the smell of his body wash drapes over me. His arm enfolds me and coax a comforting sigh from me.

"I'm sorry," I whisper to him.

"I am too." He breathes in deep. "Go to sleep, Fallon," he whispers, the exhaustion overtaking his voice.

CHAPTER THIRTY-THREE

I enjoy the chill of the night as I sit on the back porch in a rocker that I feel right at home in. It came as part of a pair, and Jesse will sometimes sit out here with me. We will watch the sunset or sit in full silence, just comfortable with each other's presence.

As if he's sensed my thoughts, he appears from around the corner with a blanket and mug in his hand. He hands me the blanket and puts the cup of what smells like the good coffee on the table in between the rockers.

"Mom sent that out here. She thought you might like it." He nods towards the mug.

I nod, still watching the sunset, feeling his eyes linger on my face. He understands me well enough to know something is on my mind.

"Are you going to tell me what last night was about?" he asks in a voice laced with concern. I'm sure if I dared to look at his face, I would be able to see the unmistakable look of worry visible in every feature.

I stare out into the night, fireflies lighting up the yard. It brings a little satisfaction to my soul to watch something that was so enchanting as a child. But unfortunately for me, it doesn't clear my thoughts.

I sigh as I prepare to voice them. "You called your ex . . . I don't even know what Shady is to you."

"She's not someone you need to worry about."

"Do *not* tell me not to worry about it. You had her babysitting me. I get that you want to protect me, Jesse, but that was going too far." I stand up and walk over to the railing, grabbing it so hard I can feel a splinter of wood digging into my palm.

I hear his footsteps before I feel him come up behind me. He encases me between his arms as he slides his hands down to my wrist, rubbing circles on the insides. He reaches up to sweep my hair behind my ear, something that usually comforts me. Tonight, it just hurts.

"And you getting into that car with Jordan and racing wasn't? God Fallon, so many things could have happened to you on that track!" His forehead drops to my shoulder, and he takes a long deep breath.

I feel his sigh breeze across my neck. He lifts his head as I turn to face him, pain evident on his face.

I let out my own breath. I shouldn't have gotten into Jordan's car. I was just so damn angry at Jesse. Or maybe I was really just angry at myself. I hadn't really decided which one it was just yet, but I did know one thing: I needed some kind of closure.

"Jess, your Dad is calling a meeting in the office." Cason rounds the corner, and instantly tenses when he sees us.

"Sorry, man, he wasn't taking No for an answer. I tried to talk him out of it."

Jesse drops his head and closes his eyes, pinching his nose. "Yeah, tell him I'll be right there."

"He doesn't want you. He wants to see her." Cason points in my direction.

Jesse's head snaps up at the same time that I spit out, "What?"

"Yeah, man. He asked for Fallon," Cason winces. My stomach clenches. This can't be good.

"Why would he want to talk to me?" I ask him.

"I'm not sure. He doesn't . . . I mean, he can't . . ." Jesse's loss for words worries me.

"Isn't it obvious?" Cason interrupts.

"What do you mean?" Jesse lets out a frustrated growl.

"She shows up, and all of a sudden, we have shit going down. He's looking at her like she's the problem."

Jesse tenses at his words and grits out, "What are you trying to say?"

198

Cason throws up his hands. "I'm not saying it's her fault. You know I want to take those bastards down just as much as you. I don't blame Fallon for that—that all started a long time before she arrived. I'm just saying this is what he sees. He sees her as a weakness."

"Then we show him she's not." Jesse's stern gaze meets Cason's.

Cason doesn't hesitate, "And we sure as shit will. But today, we just need to get her through a meeting with your dad."

Jesse and I walk through the office door hand-in-hand with Cason behind us.

Jesse's father scowls as we enter. "I see you brought the entire gang with you. You boys may leave. I don't need your presence here to speak with Miss Blake."

"I think I'll stay." Jesse stands tall and firm as Cason crosses his arms.

"Look at you three. Living under my roof, eating my food, and this is how you show your respect? Tell me, Miss Blake, are you the cause of my son's sudden need to rebel?" His father motions to me, and that is when I notice the same swirling tattoo as Jesse's peaking up from under the rolled-up sleeve of his dress shirt. I push the idea that Jesse got a tattoo just to please his father to the back of my mind as I step forward, standing shoulder to shoulder with Jesse. There is one thing I will not let him do: he's not going to stand here and make me the problem in the relationship he has with his son.

"With all due respect, sir, you know nothing about me. Whatever you think you know because you read a file that some background check provided has nothing to do with who I am." I hold this man's stare, even though I have no respect for someone who will treat his own child as poorly as he treats Jesse. Jesse is a business transaction, an heir to this man's kingdom, and nothing more. I can see it in the way he looks at him. I understand why Jesse has built such a hardness in his core.

Mr. Callaway levels me with a stare that has my insides quivering. It's the same stare Jesse has when he's in command mode.

"I know enough. It doesn't surprise me that my son almost got himself arrested for hitting a man that started stirring up trouble for me around the same time you arrived." He nods in Jesse's direction.

"He was attacking her." Jesse's fists are balled at his side, and he starts forward, grinding out something unintelligible. I catch his arm to stop him, and he looks back at me.

I shake my head to him. "Don't."

I walk forward and place my hands on the desk before me. My expression is downright lethal. This man is hurting my family. But even more, he is standing in the way of justice. His eyes harden when he looks at my face.

Time to get my point across.

"That pretty little file you have. I bet it told you my full name, age, maybe even mentioned that I dated Marcus. It probably told you I had a baby that died, father unknown, but with the timelines, I'm sure you guessed Marcus was the father. I would almost bet that you had a copy of Luna's death certificate in your hands within a week of my presence around around your son. I'd even bet that you have all of my mother's records as well. That is what a man of power does right? But did your files tell you that I had a stillborn birth because Marcus beat the shit out of me with the intention of killing our child?"

Oh, this man is so good at masking his features, but he has the same eyes as his sons—the ones that tell all if you know what you're looking for. I see the glimmer of surprise even though he schools his expression to maintain the stern look of disgust.

"Your records probably tell you I fell down the stairs in my home." A sick, distorted laugh falls out of my mouth. "The funny part of it all is that I didn't even have stairs in my home. We lived in an apartment on the bottom floor." I shake my head, trying to pull my thoughts together.

"He was there at the hospital by my side, with a gun in his waistband. Threatening me, threatening my family, if I so much as tried to tell anyone that the bruises covering my pregnant belly weren't from a stair but from the bottom of his boot that he repeatedly pounded into me." I hear the faint hiss from behind me, realizing Jesse didn't know how bad it really was. I close my eyes for a minute. Reliving the nightmare reignites the heaviness that I have worked so hard to push away.

"You don't have to trust me, and I really don't give a damn if you like me, but there are two things you need to understand about me at this moment. The first is that I do not dance around a problem and pretend it doesn't exist. I get it, you don't want me here, and if it weren't for your wife I probably wouldn't be allowed to stay in this house. And the second? There is nothing I want more than to see Marcus suffer for everything he has done to me, because of me. That is my goal. If you're taking down Jax, and bringing down Marcus? Well, Mr. Callaway, I'm all in. But I won't allow you to berate your son. Because everything he has done has been to make you proud of him."

I take a few moments to observe James Callaway. I want to be sure it sinks in. His resolve falters for a moment at the mention of his son. He didn't realize how close Jesse and I have become. I've just confirmed that I'm not going anywhere, and that is a problem for him.

"Jesse, leave us." He turns to his son.

"No fucking way." Jesse places himself slightly in front of me, his shoulder brushing against mine.

"I said *leave*," Mr. Callaway grinds out. His scowl fills the room with the irritation that his son is rebelling against him.

I watch Jesse's fist form, and I cover his hand in mine as I pull his face to mine. I try to give him my bravest look, but I can tell he isn't buying it.

"Go," I whisper, and he starts shaking his head. I stop him by placing my other hand on his face. "It's okay. Go."

His eyes narrow. I give him an encouraging smile. It falters a bit, but it's enough to convince him.

"I'll be right outside. You so much as holler, I'm breaking that fucking door down." He brings his hand to swipe the hair back from my face.

He turns his head towards his father, and if looks could kill, Jesse's burning his father down, but he lets me go and turns toward the door. He only glances back at me once more before the click of the door shutting reverberates through the room.

Or maybe that is just my heart beating entirely too hard.

"It doesn't take a genius to figure out you're the reason for my son's defiance," James says as he drops down into his chair. He motions to the chair behind me as well. "Please have a seat. I wouldn't want my son to burn my office down because I didn't go through the pleasantries."

I remain standing. I don't blink at his jab at me. Shaking my head, I say, "For a man that is as business savvy as you are, you are blind as a father."

He props his feet up on his desk and glares at me from his chair. "Please, Miss Blake, enlighten me."

I laugh, and it comes out sardonic. "You raised him to be a leader, but you forgot one important part."

"And what is that?" His amusement is written on his face.

"He's still just a boy who wants to please his father. I'm guessing you weren't banking on that being a problem with him, or having it turn into resentment towards you."

"That may be so, but given the circumstances, I only see one thing stopping him from fulfilling his role here. He'll be stronger in the end for it." He brings his feet down to the floor as he leans forward, giving me a hard stare. "I'm a businessman, Miss Blake, and I think we have an opportunity for a business deal. I'm willing to partner with you and my son on this. You're right, Jax and all of his gang need to be brought down. They are causing trouble in the town. But what I won't allow is for you to bring my son down with it. I hear your mom is about to get out of the hospital. Where do you plan on living?"

We have nowhere to go. He knows we don't. Our house was burned to the ground. The only thing we have is my mom's car. Dread fills me.

"I didn't think you had anywhere to go. I will provide housing and an allowance for amenities. I will even provide any medical necessities for your mother during her recovery. I can offer her a full-time position at Callaway Exports that will pay much more than her minimum-wage job cleaning offices. Once she is back on her feet, of course."

At what price would I pay to deal with the devil? I cross my arms. "And the catch?"

"You leave. You leave Jesse and my daughter alone as soon as Jax and Marcus are brought down, and you don't bring my children down whatever hole you crawled out of."

I'm astonished that after everything I've just said he thinks he can buy me. He wants me to leave Jesse. He may be offering everything we need on a silver platter, but I would never betray my friends, my family, like that.

"Think about it. You can go." He stands up and places a few files in his briefcase, dismissing me like I'm a peasant.

"Fallon, I don't need to remind you that this offer is only valid as long as it stays between you and me. Neither Jesse nor Jade need to know." I turn back to him. The anger I have towards this man and his manipulation goes beyond my initial expectations.

"You are a dumb man, James," I say to him. But for such a dumb man, he sure knows a lot about Jax and Marcus, even me. I should've expected that, he is Jesse's father, but it's still unnerving to know he's watching.

I walk through the door to where my heart is, leaving the door wide open to show this man precisely what he's up against. Two people willing to fight for each other, even with someone so close.

CHAPTER THIRTY-FOUR

It's finally the weekend, and after this long week I want nothing more than to blow off some steam. We all need to relax some, and there is a party at another ball player's house. It's just the thing the boys need, so we all get ready for a long night out. The party is in a barn behind his house. We have to park on the grass and walk up with our phones out for light to see where we are stepping. I could see people dancing through the barn doors, and the music is blaring. I guess being out in a field means the music can be as loud as you want.

We walk into the barn, and before we can spot the ice chest full of beer, Cason's already dragging out four beers.

"Do you see Adam anywhere? He was supposed to meet us," Jade asks. I look around, but don't spot Adam. I do find a furious Elizabeth staring our direction. I roll my eyes and turn to Cason as he walks over, handing us all a beer. I pop the top, taking a long pull from the can.

"Woah, now that's the spirit, Fallon!" Cason raises his beer to salute me before chugging it down.

I look around until I find a wooden bench off to the side and get Jesse and Jade's attention to sit there.

Jade shakes her head, "I'm gonna walk around to see if I can find Adam."

"Okay, good luck!" I look toward the crowd. I won't be wandering around too much. I sit down on the bench and lean back on the wall, content to just watch everyone.

"I'm gonna go take a piss. Sit tight with Cason, I'll be back." Jesse whisper-yells in my ear. I nod to let him know I heard him, and he places a kiss on my forehead before letting Cason know where he's going. Cason sits next to me. He seems to be deep in thought, which I find odd as Cason is usually the life of the party.

"What's going on, Case?" I bump my shoulder into his. "Don't have enough women to choose from?"

Cason chuckles, but his smile doesn't reach his eyes. "Nah, I'm not digging the women tonight. But I do want to ask you something."

I lift an eyebrow, wondering what he could possibly need to ask me. "Sure. What is it?"

"Does it get better? When you lost Luna . . . does the ache go away?"

I consider his question, guessing it has everything to do with his mom. When we woke up the next morning after rescuing her from The Depot she was gone. There wasn't a note, nothing, she was just gone. I reach over, wrapping my arm around his waist and putting my head on his shoulder. "I wish I could tell you it does. But the answer is no, it doesn't go away. It stays in your core and eats at you every day. I think at some point, we just learn how to tolerate the pain, or sometimes special people can ease it."

We sit in silence just like this for a minute, but I see the wheels turning in his head. "You mean like Jesse?"

"Yes, I mean like Jesse. And Jade, and you. When I came here, I intended to hide away. To barely live, because that's how I felt—barely alive inside. But you guys, you helped me realize that living doesn't mean I'm forgetting. It just means that I have to find something to live for, and I did—in y'all."

He lets out a big breath and brings his hand up to my head, planting a kiss to my temple.

"I was gone for maybe five minutes, and you already have your hands all over my woman?" Jesse appears.

Cason smiles wide, and this time it is a little lighter. "Nah, man, it was all her. She can't keep her hands off of this." Cason stands and motions to his body. I roll my eyes, but I'm laughing with him.

"Alright, guys. I gotta go find me a woman to play with tonight." He wiggles his eyebrows as he claps Jesse on the back.

Jesse shakes his head and pulls me to him when I stand to meet him. He stares at me with a look of wonder in his eyes. I tilt my head a bit as I wrap my arms around his neck. "What?"

"You're pretty amazing, you know." His seriousness is making me squirm.

"Don't worry, you don't have to convince me to be with you." I chuckle.

He bends his knees a bit to meet me at eye level. "I'm serious. I overheard a little bit of what you said to Cason. You knew exactly what he needed to hear, and as much as I wish I could have been that person for him as his family, I'm glad you could."

"He's my family too, ya know. You all are. It just took me a little while to figure that out."

Jesse grins widely at me. "It's about time you accepted your place with us. With me."

"Yeah, yeah, come here. I'm done with the serious talk." I grab his collar and pull his lips to mine to let him know precisely what he is going to be getting later tonight. When he pulls back, he has a handsome devilish grin, and I know my message was conveyed, loud and clear.

"I'm going to get another beer. You want one?" Jesse asks as he steps back, leaving one hand around my back. I look down at my half-full beer and shake my head no. "I'm good."

He leans in and kisses the hollow of my neck before stepping away to the ice chest off to the side. He still keeps me within his view.

Jordan appears through the barn doors, scanning the crowd when his eyes land on me. He starts heading my way.

"Hey Fallon. Your girl Jade is outside on the side of the barn puking. She said to come get you."

"Jade is? Are you sure?" I ask.

"Yeah, totally. I tried to help her, but she wouldn't let me."

Mira walks up, placing her arm around Jordan's waist. "Hey, babe, there you are. I've been looking for you."

She looks at me, the moment going awkward the instant she realizes it's me standing here. "Oh. Hey, Fallon."

"Hey, Mira."

"What's going on?" she asks.

"Ah, nothing, Fallon has to go help, Jade. She's sick outside," Jordan says, but this time he seems a little fidgety.

I look over to Jesse, who is talking to one of the guys on the team. I decide not to wait for him, just in case Jade is really sick.

"Alright, I'm gonna go check on her. Let Jesse know where I'm at?"

Jordan nods, and I head outside, going through the open barn doors and peering around the building on each side. Something doesn't seem right. I slowly peek around the building, but no one is there.

"Still gullible, I see." An eerie chill runs through my body, and I immediately try to scream, but it comes out muffled when Marcus grabs me around my face and waist, muffling any sound that might come out of my mouth. I try to scream again, but I only get a big whiff of a wet, dank smell that fills my lungs and nostrils. I try to struggle against him by kicking and squirming, but he's stronger than me. He pulls me back away from the party, and even if I could scream again, no one would hear me over the music. My arms and legs are growing heavy. I keep fighting, but my limbs just won't cooperate with me. I feel dizzy. Something isn't right, and I know he's done something to me. I reach for his hand, but my arms feel like Jell-O. My world tilts, and I try to scream again. It comes out hoarse and weak, just like I feel. I have to stay awake. Every time I breathe in, my world becomes a little more unstable. Something in the back of my mind tells me to not breathe unless I have to, but my lungs react and force me pull in a deep breath. This is the one that will pull me under, of that I have no doubt. My eyes are watering, and I feel a single tear slide down my face as the world starts to fade.

"Goodnight, Fallon," Marcus whispers in my ear just as my eyelids grow heavy, and it all becomes dark.

<<<>>>

ACKNOWLEDGMENTS

This book. This book wouldn't have happened if it weren't for so many different people. I don't think the acknowledgments section is big enough for the amount of gratitude I hold in my heart for these people.

I want to start with K.R.F. Yes, girl I used those initials! You, I can't even tell you how thankful I am to have you in my life. This book wouldn't be here if you hadn't pushed me to see myself in a bigger light. But most importantly, I wouldn't be in the place that I am, have the happiness that I do, without you. You, my girl, will always be cherished by me for the impact you have had on my soul

Tara, girl you've stepped up for me in so many ways. You've been a fantastic support system and a fantastic friend. You're also the best admin I've ever had. 😊 I couldn't imagine doing this life without you and I never want to.

To my tribe, La La you're getting that tattoo. Get ready! Also, thank you all for being amazing friends. For believing in me when I didn't believe in myself and continuing to support me. Even when I talk way to much about this book. Page, thank you for letting me be you're favorite asshole. But also thank you for unconditionally being there when I need you.

Rebecca. When I started this journey, I had no idea where it would lead me. I found an editor who held my hand through writing this story. In the process you became someone I could never let go. You became the person on my good shoulder. I could never repay you the kindness that you have given me, or the therapy sessions. I truly appreciate everything about you.

Carrie, oh Carrie. Besides the fact that you make me a better writer and person. You were exactly what I needed at the right time. You challenge me in so many ways. You push me to be a better version of myself. You are the reason I am so strong today. Thank you for not giving up on me.

LitChicks, y'all are a wonderful group. I've learned so much from you all. But just the genuine understanding from you guys means so much.

My family, there are so many of you so I wont name you all. But just know that in the last six years you have all been my foundation. I could not have made it this far without you. You've each impacted my life in so many ways. You are my world, and I'm holding on to each of you for dear life.

My momma. You give me strength. I see everything you've overcome, and it empowers me. You empowered me to pursue a life where I can stand tall. One I can love. To not be afraid to fight for what I want. Because of that I found my place, as an author. You gave that to me. You gave me the strength to find me. I may not tell you enough, but my hero isn't someone famous or fictional. My hero is you.

My baby girl. You just don't know what you mean to me. I look into those baby blue eyes and know I was put on this earth to raise someone as special as you. You are my reason for it all. You give me the strive to show you what it means to be happy. To do what makes you happy. This book is proof of that. I love you.

And finally. To my Girl Gang. You have been there every step of the way even when I had nothing to offer you. I can't thank you enough for being here and supporting me to this point. Y'all are amazing!

Love you all,
Callie Rae

ABOUT THE AUTHOR

Callie Rae writes romance novels. She lives in southern Louisiana with a daughter, two furry pups, and one fat rabbit named Josie. You can find Callie in her garden pretending her thumb is green. Otherwise, she is mommin' with the best.

Instagram:@callieraeauthor
Facebook Author Page: @callieraeauthor
Website: www.authorcallierae.com

Download a FREE copy of Tagged Hearts-a second chance novella- when you join Callie Rae's newsletter. Be the first to receive updates on future releases, bonus content, and giveaways.
Sign up at https://www.authorcallierae.com

Made in the USA
Middletown, DE
11 September 2021